ACCLAIM FOR ANNE SPOLLEN'S
The Shape of Water

★ "This enchanting novel starts quietly, draws the reader in and weaves a seductive spell that holds until the last page."

—*Kirkus* (starred review)

"Riveting... Spollen's incredibly descriptive prose creates images as clear and alive as those of a master painter."

—*School Library Journal*

"Spollen's vivid writing about Magda's unusual perceptions will leave a strong impression on many teens..."

—*Booklist*

∞

Elizah Rayne is nothing like other fourteen-year-old girls. More interested in bird bones than people, she wraps herself in silence. Trying to escape the shadow of her gambler father, Elizah and her mother move into an old house that borders a cemetery. All her mother wants is for them to have "normal" lives. But that becomes impossible for Elizah when she finds a human jawbone by the river and meets Nathaniel, a strangely hypnotic boy who draws Elizah into his dreamlike and mysterious world.

Only by forgetting everything she knows can Elizah understand the truth about Nathaniel—and discover an unimaginable secret.

light beneath ferns

light beneath ferns

anne spollen

Woodbury, Minnesota

First Edition
First Printing, 2010

Book design by Steffani Sawyer
Cover design by Lisa Novak
Cover image © Claudia McKinney

Flux, an imprint of Llewellyn Publications

Library of Congress Cataloging-in-Publication Data
Spollen, Anne, 1958–
  Light beneath ferns / Anne Spollen.—1st ed.
    p. cm.
  Summary: Upon moving to her mother's upstate New York home after her gambler father leaves, ninth-grader Elizah just wants to be left alone until she meets Nathaniel in the cemetery where her mother is caretaker, and feels instantly drawn to him.
  ISBN 978-0-7387-1542-1
  [1. Supernatural—Fiction. 2. Cemeteries—Fiction. 3. Moving, Household—Fiction. 4. High schools—Fiction. 5. Schools—Fiction. 6. Ghosts—Fiction. 7. New York (State)—Fiction.] I. Title.
  PZ7.S76365Lig 2010
  [Fic]—dc22
                                    2009027509

Flux
Llewellyn Publications
A Division of Llewellyn Worldwide, Ltd.
2143 Wooddale Drive, Dept. 978-0-7387-1542-1
Woodbury, MN 55125-2989, U.S.A.
www.fluxnow.com

Printed in the United States of America

*This novel is dedicated, with much love,
to my son Christopher, who has always shown me
that the power of silence is its ability to speak.*

"Do you remember how electrical currents and 'unseen waves' were laughed at? The knowledge about man is still in its infancy."
—Albert Einstein

not the first chapter

This story does not teach a lesson. It does not explain gravity or the pack rituals of wolves or how the sun will explode one day and leave us all inside a gray welt of ice and famine. It will not make you popular or get you invitations to parties, if you are after that sort of thing. If death and the dead make you afraid, you better just stop reading and go take a nap. If bones scare you, you cannot read this book. At all. Because really, things started happening just a little after I found that bone.

You should also know that this story doesn't begin at the beginning. Really, nothing does. And don't believe people who tell you that's how the world works. My story goes sideways, like all stories. I pick the parts that I want to be the beginning, the middle, and the end because nothing ever happens in order; we just pretend it does. Everything happens more like a rainstorm with wind and lightning and confusion all happening at once, and none of it is divided into sections.

I am not going to tell you a lot about me in the beginning like other girl narrators because I am nothing like other girl narrators. If you were smart enough to find this book, and find me, you can figure out how I am without being told. But I will tell you what I am not.

I don't live on a prairie or in the American West or before, during, or after any war that you would find in a history book. I don't like flowers, or save small animals; I don't have whimsical adventures that end neatly with a moral. I don't locate lost children. In fact, I'm not even fond of small children. I don't solve mysteries or fix what's broken. I don't scare easily, but I am not noble in the least. Usually, when stuff scares me, I avoid it. I also don't believe in courage. I think it is a radically misunderstood, applauded form of suicide. And I don't wish I lived anywhere else, even though we live on the edge of a graveyard.

The graveyard, Wenspaugh Rural Cemetery, is in my mother's hometown in upstate New York (or at least, in the town she moved to when she was about nine years old). When we moved back, she got a job as the cemetery care-taker. Some people live on the edge of a lake or a town or a meadow. We live on the edge of a cemetery.

You're thinking, "Oh, she lives on the edge of a cemetery and that's how and why she found the bone." And I already warned you that stories do not go in order like that. The graveyard, in the end, had nothing to do with me finding the bone.

Not a thing.

september

The high school is being painted so we have to go to the elementary school for ninth grade registration. The hallways have that ghosted, vacant feel of late summer with boxes towered high and a yellowish, drifting scent of wax. The classrooms are painted in colors so bright and glossy that the walls seem to chirp. And, unlike my old school, almost every classroom has a birdcage hanging from one corner. There are no birds in the cages today; there are no kids either. I try not to think how the kids are like the birds, only instead of cages, the kids are locked into classrooms.

The next day, the high school has the same smell as the elementary school, only the classrooms are not painted as brightly and there are no birdcages. Each day, the smell grows fainter. I follow my schedule during those first two weeks, while the smell of newness fades, managing to speak only a few words. Then in science, in the middle of the third week, Ms. Poulle calls on me.

"Elizah." She says this in a bright, expectant voice, and I wonder what, exactly, will happen to me if I don't answer. But she doesn't pause to wait for me. "Elizah, please turn around and face me." I continue looking out the window toward the mountains that hem Wenspaugh. I notice dark patches with jagged edges on the mountain face, and I realize the patches are clouds overhead, blocking the sun.

"Elizah," she says again. "Since we are discussing community and habitat, it would be interesting if you could offer some comment on how you see us as a community here in Wenspaugh. It's not often we get to feast on new blood here."

I like that she used the word *blood*, but I still don't want to answer her.

"You see, Elizah, the quiet students always intrigue me," Ms. Poulle says as she walks right over to me, eclipsing my view of the outside. "I always wonder what's going on with them. There has to be *something* going on inside all that quietness. Nature abhors a vacuum, Elizah, and so do I. So, what so far has stricken you about Wenspaugh, about us, our schools? Because sometimes it's so difficult to see how we appear to others, isn't that right?"

She waits.

"So what do you think of us, Elizah?"

I have no choice but to answer, with her standing over me, and I remember the birds trapped in cages. So I tell Ms. Poulle about the birdcages down at the elementary school and my theory of how students are chained inside school rooms like those birds, and how looking at the mountains right now reminds me of those cages because they are surrounding us.

"Well, Elizah, that's an interesting take. I do think all of us live inside a cage of some kind or another. Maybe the trick is not minding your cage so much. Or maybe even liking it."

I look back outside after she walks away, waiting for the bell to ring for lunch. Normally at lunch, I sit in a corner of the cafeteria and do homework so I can have time to myself after school. Only that day, a group of girls from the class comes up to me at lunch and begins telling me what a good question they thought I gave Ms. Poulle, and acting like I want to discuss something with them. I remind them that it was a statement, not a question; then I endure their laughter.

"She is like the weirdest teacher in the school, Ms. Poulle," Brittany, clearly the alpha girl of the pack, says. She touches my shoulder as she says this, the white tips of her manufactured nail tips grazing me. "You know, she keeps pig babies in jars in that room. Can you imagine? Pig babies. Clearly the weirdest teacher."

"She has one pig fetus," I remind Brittany. "She's a science teacher. She's supposed to have it. It would only be weird if she had a pig fetus in formaldehyde and she was teaching French."

"Oh, she's just odd is all," Brittany says, ignoring logic. The two girls next to her, slightly smaller Brittany replications, laugh. At that moment, a lunch monitor comes over to me with a pass to Mrs. Daytner's office.

"Use the exit under the clock," the woman says to me. "And no talking in the hallways."

"Right," I say, since I have spoken maybe seventy-five words since the first day of school three weeks ago.

The guidance office is near a bank of windows, and I stand there watching clouds bang into the mountains until a custodian snarls something at me about making smudges on the glass. I enter, wondering why these places always have a hushed, muted feel, like entering a fish tank.

Mrs. Daytner is waiting for me at the threshold of her private office. "You must be Elizah Rayne."

I look at her. She is tall and narrow with a small round head. She reminds me of an inverted exclamation point. Thinking this, I smile and say, "Yes. I'm Elizah Rayne."

She ushers me in and we sit across from one another. No one says anything for a few seconds.

Mrs. Daytner's hands are folded on her pale blue desk blotter. Two rows of plants obediently bloom behind her. Through the window behind her, I see kids playing soccer out on the field. Everything orderly, everything predictable. "Well, you know why you're here, don't you, Elizah?"

"This is a counseling office," I say. "So I would assume it's for counseling of some kind."

"Yes. Wenspaugh is a difficult place in many ways," Mrs. Daytner says. "Many of these students, most in fact, have been together since kindergarten. I would imagine it's difficult for a quiet student to make friends here." Her hair is cut so when she angles her head, it moves together in one jaw-length chunk. I think about how the kids in this school move together in one group, in one force, like a wave traveling around the ocean. When you think about it, waves never go anywhere. They just loop and loop around the globe, all connected and blunt in force, and they never leave the ocean except to go up into the atmosphere to do the same thing again. And again.

A meteorite travels alone.

So does a falling star.

And you remember them.

"What are you thinking about right now, Elizah?"

She waits. A ticking sound fills the air. Even the kids on the field stop moving.

"Elizah?"

"I'm thinking how I want to call you Mrs. Daytime instead of Mrs. Daytner. It suits you more."

She smiles. "That's fine, if that's how you want to establish control. Tell me, Elizah, are you finding it difficult here, the adjustment?"

"Not really. But my mother thinks I am. She told me she was going to call you. Well, not you, specifically. She just said someone at the school. To help me with the transition and all."

Daytime nods, and I notice small rills of darkness around each of her nostrils. I keep staring at the darkness staining the paleness of her skin. "Your mother is very worried about you."

"Did she say what she's worried about? Specifically?"

"Well, it's the same as what your teachers have been telling me. You are very quiet in school, Elizah. Sort of detached socially. Molly, ah, your mother, mentioned that you said you don't intend to make any friends here. Made a statement to that effect."

We watch each other for a few more seconds. "Have you met my mother?"

"Not in person. We've emailed each other and spoken twice on the phone."

I nod. The bell rings, and it occurs to me that talking to her might be a good way to miss the first half of English. "My mother is not exactly the belle of the ball, you know. She goes shopping at four o'clock in the morning at the all-night supermarket so she doesn't have to see anyone. And she did all her Christmas shopping on the Internet."

"Right. So she's in a position to understand your social anxiety."

"Is that what I have? Because I'm quiet?"

Daytime gives me this tiny twist of a smile, as if she is sucking on a lemon and has just come to a particularly tart spot. "I think, most likely, you have some form of social anxiety, yes."

"So do extroverts have something wrong with them, too? You know, like a lack of boundaries?"

"What do you mean?"

"I mean ... what I mean is the way they prattle on and on, mostly about themselves, what has happened to them, what they think, all of that even when you don't want to listen. And even if you're clear about not wanting to listen. You can look away or up at the ceiling and they keep going. They lack a filter that tells them when their audience is exhausted by them. Maybe it's some form of social compulsion to just talk on and on like that. Maybe extroverts could use a little social anxiety."

Daytime sighs. "Elizah. I'm here to help."

"I'm being serious. And why don't I feel anxious if I have social anxiety? Why do I feel normal?"

"It becomes normal after a certain amount of time. Or you think it's normal. It's not easy to move to a new state, to begin school where you don't know anyone. So maybe being silent feels normal to you."

"So, can anything become normal after a certain amount of time? Anything at all?"

"Not anything. I meant certain behaviors. In a way, we all become accustomed to ourselves, to our routines, to our modes of being. One of the benefits of counseling is to make you more aware of your... well..." She laughs, a dry little breath closer to gasping than breathing. "Of your patterns. And we all have patterns."

"Like wolves."

"Excuse me?"

"Never mind."

Daytime looks down at her paperwork. "I'd like to meet with you once a week beginning next week, but first I have to ask you a few questions. Let me just find my list here."

I don't believe the whole thing she said about patterns and getting used to them. Not at all. During the three weeks before we moved, time traveled backwards and sideways and none of it felt normal. We floated inside an underwater place where nothing seemed real. That was probably because after my father left, we adopted the sleep/wake cycle of hamsters.

At ten in the morning, my mother and I went to bed with the curtains drawn against the sun, and the phone on the battery charger so it couldn't ring. We got up at six o'clock in the evening with the curtains still drawn. We kept putting our things in boxes and moving the boxes into the garage, except we were still living in the house, emptying it piece by piece until the garage grew impacted and lightless with towers of boxes. Our space, where we had once lived our lives, grew vacant as a canyon.

On one of those mornings, my mother looked at me and whispered, "The movers will come after we are in Wenspaugh." We were sitting on the kitchen floor at dawn. We were having dinner. I remember thinking, I cannot say goodbye to anyone here, not my friends, not my teachers, no one. I have become a living ghost in the place where I was born, in the only place I have ever known.

All because of what my father had done.

"Elizah," Daytime says, interrupting my memory, "it says here on the form that your father is not living with you. And your mother is not sure where he is. Is that right?" She opens her eyes very wide as she says this.

"If it's on the form, it must be true."

"I see. Perhaps we can begin here." Daytime taps her pen on the form. "Tell me, how does that make you feel, that your father is not living with you?"

"I guess I feel all right."

"I'm not sure what 'all right' means, Elizah."

"It means shit happens." I wait for Daytime's expression to change after I say that, but she keeps sitting there, her eyes still open wide as if she is slowly, silently being electrocuted. I sort of like that thought so I smile.

"Yes, it certainly does happen." She smiles back at me. "But what do you mean right now by saying that—that it happens?"

"I mean it doesn't matter how I feel. How I feel won't change what happens or what did happen."

Daytime dims her eyes to show understanding, and I remember this animal documentary we saw in science last year about behaviors that are supposed to make the other animals not afraid of you. Daytime dims her eyes in a way that reminds me of a wolf exposing an underbelly.

"Maybe," Daytime says with her eyes all soft, "you could tell me how you feel about not knowing where your dad is."

"All I know is we don't know if he's dead or away. Mom says he is living inside darkness."

"Living inside darkness. What do you feel when you think of that image? Does it worry you?"

"I think he's probably all right. Worms live inside darkness all the time and they do just fine."

"Worms. I see. Do you miss your father?"

I shrug my shoulders. "It's like he was never around when I was little. Not that much or anything, and now that he's missing, it's like, doncha miss him, Elizah, well, doncha? Like it's not all right not to miss him. Or I don't miss him enough, or something."

Daytime puts her pen down. "It is perfectly fine not to miss him, Elizah. Emotions do not have a right or a wrong." She keeps looking at me. "Elizah, where do you think your father is? Just a guess now."

"Probably on an Indian reservation."

"Why would you say that?"

"Because gambling is legal there."

ගිං

The next day at lunch, Brittany and her friends come over to me while I am reading.

"So what happened in the counseling office?" Brittany asks. Her eyelashes remind me of spider legs, mascara freezing each one into a curve that delicately arcs into the air, like a spider leg extending out from a web.

"She taught me how to say *Go Away* in seven different languages."

This makes Brittany and her friends go all electric with laughter. I get up and go to the bathroom, where I spend the remainder of the period watching water drip through a liver-colored patch on the ceiling. For the rest of the day, whenever I see Brittany or any of her satellites, they smile and wink at me in a way that makes them look as if they're recovering from exposure to nerve gas.

ගිං

That night, before dinner, while the kitchen fills with heavy, golden light, my mother asks me about Daytime. "She called and said you had your first session yesterday. How was it?"

"Mostly we talked about worms."

My mother looks out the window. "I wish you would let people help you."

"I don't want help." Mom keeps looking out the window, looking up at the trees that line the entrance to the cemetery. They are tall and filled with amber leaves that have a strange kind of ripeness to them, as if in dying they've discovered an enhanced level of energy.

I watch my mother from the wideboard kitchen table. She still hasn't turned to face me. "I don't see why I need to sit there and talk to that plank."

"She is not a plank. She is a perfectly bright and balanced woman with an interest in the paranormal. She told me this cemetery is haunted."

"Oh, now that's original. A haunted cemetery. Words from a plank."

"Elizah, she's there to help."

"She doesn't know me. How could she possibly want to help me?"

My mother turns from the window, blinks for a few minutes, then moves a box onto the floor. Most of our stuff is still in boxes from the move. We just circle around them, and every time we open them, we look inside at the jars and spoons and magazines, then close the flaps again. This is how we packed, my mother and I, over those three weeks—like peasants fleeing a scourge of plague. Shirts in with food, socks and slippers lining boxes of photographs, soap in with the sheets.

"Mrs. Daytner told me there's a man named Jonas Martleby who walks around the cemetery." Mom's eyebrows go up as she says this; it's the face she used to make when I was little and she thought something was scary.

I look at my mother, standing there moving boxes around without accomplishing anything. She has glasses on top of her head, and glasses hanging from a chain on her neck, and she still sees nothing.

"I cannot imagine anything more thrilling than seeing a ghost or a spirit. What an amazing idea." She takes two bowls out of a box filled with sweaters, then closes the box again.

"So he's a ghost, this Jonas? People have seen him?"

"Apparently. I, personally, have never seen him, mind you, but Ella says there have been all kinds of reports that people have seen him walking around the cemetery. I don't think I would be scared if I saw a ghost or a spirit; I think I would be really kind of excited."

"At least most people would leave me alone if I were dead."

Mom puts the two bowls inside the box again. "Now, Elizah, what kind of statement, exactly, is that? What am I supposed to think of that now? You tell me."

"The trouble, Mom, is that I don't want to hang out with any of the kids here. I like to be alone. And that seems to be a problem here in Wenspaugh. I just don't have any interest in knowing the people in my school." I get up and start clearing the table.

"You should have friends. Everyone needs friends." My mother takes a second box down and leaves it next to the first.

"You have no friends, Mom. I hate to break it to you."

"I'm going to get friends, though. Mrs. Daytner invited me to join a paranormal group she's a member of, and I said yes. I even offered to host some of the events here. I want friends, now. Now that..." She rubs the chain holding her glasses as if it's an amulet. What she doesn't say is, now that Dad is gone, now that we have a chance at a normal life. Instead, she pats the top of the second box and goes into the living room where she turns the radio on so she doesn't have to think about anything that's already happened, or how we can't fix it.

river, leaves

The next Saturday morning it's warm and my mother is sitting at her computer when I walk into the living room. She looks up at me. "Remember I told you I joined that paranormal group Ella Daytner belongs to?"

"Yeah. So they found ghosts inside your computer? Is that why you're telling me?"

"Stop. We're going to have a meeting of people interested in the paranormal. I'm hosting it."

I smile. "Do they know you have the social habits of octopi living in a cave?"

"Stop, Elizah. I'm trying to change all that. By the way, Mrs. Daytner is one of the people coming. Ella Daytner. She's a lovely person. Oh, when we spoke yesterday, she told me about your assignment."

I pull my favorite green shirt out of a box filled with canned tomatoes.

"Daytime cannot give me an assignment. She's not a teacher."

"All she asked is if you could just think of reasons you want to be alone and you guys could talk about them at your next session. Just think about it, Elizah. You say you like to be alone, and she wants to know if you can say why you prefer it. That shouldn't be hard."

I nod. "Fine." I put one of my mother's soy-flour pancakes onto a plate and sit on the couch near her desk.

"So you'll think about why you aren't making any friends or speaking to anyone in school?"

"Yup."

But I already know the answer. I need to be quiet now because other people feel like clutter. I like silence, and long afternoons where I sit watching the river and listening to dogs bark in the distance. And while I'm quiet, I have this strange sense that I'm preparing for something I can't name.

But I will never say this to Daytime. Instead, I'll make something up. I like to lie to people who think they can find truths. Like truth is that easy to exhume.

My mother frowns at the computer screen, then whispers something toward the keyboard.

"It's not enchanted, you know, that computer. It won't listen."

"I know that." She clicks her mouse three times in a row. "Elizah, Mrs. Daytner says she also wants you to think of positive interests that you have. You know, things you like to participate in."

"Being alone."

"Aside from that." My mother taps the *enter* key, then curses very softly.

I like bones. I wonder if I can tell Daytime that. I particularly like bird bones. When my father was still around, we hunted for fallen birds. He knew how to submerge the bodies in an acid solution so the feathers soaked off, but the bones, particularly the wing bones, my favorites, stayed intact. Wing bones are incredibly delicate, and incredibly intricate at the same time. When you hold them up to the sky, they look like they are in flight. Wing bones are prizes. So when we found a bird, my father would dunk it into a vat and save the bones for me.

After I painted the bones, my mother and I would brush clear varnish over the paint and make jewelry. The wing bones made the most beautiful pieces: thinly delicate as veins, they looked like pieces of fire falling from the sky. I have close to fifty brooches made from bird bones, but I don't make them anymore even though there are a lot of dead birds around the edges of this graveyard. My mother thinks that's because they can smell death in the soil.

"I'll tell her how much I like bones, Mom. There's an interest."

My mother leans over from the desk and tries to poke me in the side with her finger. "No. You can't tell her that, and you know it. Elizah, do you ever think about how I don't need you to make all this more difficult than it already is for me?"

For her. Because for me, it's all so easy.

"Why can't I tell her about the bones?"

"Elizah." Mom clicks at the keyboard, then turns to look at me. "Bones are probably not the best subject for a girl who lives on cemetery property to discuss. People will think it's weird, that you're weird, that we're odd people. And that's precisely what we don't want. We had enough of that in Queensport."

"Oh, okay. So if I don't talk about bones, no one will think of me as weird. Is that all I have to do? Wow, life is much easier now that we've moved. Much, much easier."

"There you go, Elizah, making things more complicated than they have to be."

"Right. So I pretend I'm into … like, scrapbooking or stuffed animals. I basically lie so people will like me. I got it now, Mom."

My mother shakes her head back and forth several times, but says nothing.

"Bones," my mother says finally, "make most people upset."

"So it's not okay that I like bones?"

"I'm not saying that. Just, please, Elizah, think of something else."

I am not a girl who is squeamish about bones.

Please.

So maybe on that Saturday morning, right after sitting on the couch eating soy pancakes with honey and organic blueberries, telling my mother how I might tell Daytime how much I liked bones, maybe on that day, it all began.

Maybe.

Or maybe it began decades ago when the owner of the bone died.

I don't know. No one does.

Anyway, after I wash the breakfast dishes and my mother arranges for a medium to come to her paranormal meeting, our doorbell rings. When we lived in Queensport, my parents ignored the doorbell, and the phone. They would just keep putting towels into the linen closet or reading the newspaper while the people stood on the front stoop or the phone rang on and on.

"It's our house," they would say. "No one has the right to ring a bell and demand our time like that."

Neighbors would look at us unloading groceries from the car the way most people would look at aliens debarking from a pod. Even waving was out of the question.

But here my mother has to answer the door; she would lose her job if she didn't, and we would lose our rent-free house. That morning, while I'm getting dressed, I overhear the conversation, and I can tell there are genealogists talking to my mother.

Genealogists are always coming to the graveyard to trace their families. They sit for hours in the tiny front office, not minding the stained, orange-cushioned furniture that the town historical society donated. They sit reading death certificates and drinking coffee. Part of my mother's job is to guide them in their search for graves.

I go outside, into the bright parch of the day, and walk the short distance to the riverbank, close to the oldest section of the graveyard. From here, I can look up into the Shawangunk Mountains where everything burns golden and red. The slow violin of river runs, water sighing over rocks. People in canoes and kayaks, some of them from my school, drift downriver, and when I see them approaching, I lurk behind a boulder so I don't have to talk. I'm doing exactly this, crouching behind the boulder, while two girls from my gym class paddle past me. Their hair, blond and long, is braided and for a minute I smile: Pocahontas gone Nordic.

In my squatting position, my knees start to ache a little so I plop down butt-first, digging my heels into the soil. I look over to see my mother pointing to the nearly abandoned graves in the northernmost corner of the grave-yard while the genealogists listen. My heel hits something solid, and I reach down to move the stick and that is when I see it, half covered in the wet, reddish mud that flanks the river.

Except I do not know this is a bone: it looks like a piece of branch, and I immediately like its shape. It reminds me of a bird wing, so I take a scatter of leaves and rub them against the bone to clean off the mud. That's when I see that the stick is not a stick. It's lighter in color and shaped perfectly.

I carry the bone with me back to the house, where I stash it in a paper bag under the sink. The genealogists look up at me as I pass, and I think, once you finish your research, I will begin mine. I don't dare think yet that the bone might be human.

I don't dare.

☙❧

My mother is sitting at the kitchen table when I come in. "What were you doing down by the river before? I saw you there, crouched like a cougar."

"There were girls from my school canoeing down the river. I didn't want to talk to them." I wash my hands at the sink, careful to pull the left side of my jacket out of my mother's line of vision so she doesn't ask what is bulging inside my pocket. I like the lightly firm way the bone presses against my hip, delicate and solid at the same time.

"Do you suppose," my mother asks as she rises from the table, "that the girls wanted to talk to you?"

"I don't know. Probably."

"So then. Think about what you did, your first response. You crouch behind the boulder like an animal, either one who hunts or is hunted…"

"Wait," I interrupt. "That's kind of a huge distinction. Hunter or hunted…"

"My point," my mother says, walking over to the small kitchen island, "is that you were behaving by using your animal instincts instead of your human reason. I would think that a girl who is so good at biology, who likes science so much, would rely more on her powers of reason."

"People can surprise you every day."

She begins to make me a peanut butter sandwich. I want to tell her that I can do that myself now, but it's kind of a ritual at this point, my mother making me a peanut butter sandwich while we sit and talk. I take my usual seat at the table and wait for her.

"My point, Elizah, is very simple. Most likely those girls would just wave to you and move on down the river. Do you think they would stop, pull the canoe onto land, and start a conversation with you? Or would they just wave?"

"It doesn't matter. I just don't want them to know my spot."

"Your spot." My mother squints at me and shakes her head slightly from side to side, as if this gesture will clarify what I have just said. I have seen her strike this exact posture when trying to speak to people who don't understand English.

"My spot on the river. I don't want them to expect to see me there. I don't want to share anything with them."

"Not even a wave?"

"Nope."

"That's how you feel right now. You may feel differently when you get used to the area." Mom motions outside. "The leaves are changing." She comes over to the table with my sandwich. "I forgot how much earlier they change now that we're north." She puts the plate down, and her eyes are still gazing outside when she says, "You know, there was something else when I was speaking to Mrs. Daytner. She has some real concerns about you."

"Wait. How did you just go from the leaves to Daytime?"

My mother sighs. "I don't know, Elizah. I guess the leaves reminded me of how the mountains looked when I lived up here as a kid, and then I thought of school and how you've been in school for a month now, and I thought of my conversation with Mrs. Daytner."

I nod. "So what are her concerns?"

"She thinks you have social issues. Pretty obvious ones."

"I know that. So did you tell her I'm being raised by someone who goes grocery shopping at four a.m. at the all-night market to avoid seeing people or knowing what they eat? Did you ever tell her how you hate looking at what's in people's carts because it makes you imagine their lives after they leave the supermarket, and you can't stand that? Because that's, like, outgoing, Mom."

Mom smirks. "Elizah, the beauty of being out of school is that I no longer have to be nice to people or even be around them if I don't want to be. And don't you think Mrs. Daytner understands that a woman who chooses to be the caretaker of an old graveyard is not exactly going to be invited to the Garden Club lunch? She's not an idiot."

"You didn't talk to her long enough." I take a bite of my sandwich. Mom is still smiling, standing over me, hunched like a bear.

"Anyway, here's another thing: she wants you to go to Mary Alice's Halloween party in a couple of weeks."

"I'm sure Daytime wants a lot of things for me," I say after swallowing. "But I'd rather be dead than go to Mary Alice's party. I heard Beth Mooney talking about it on the bus. It's going to be a sleepover and..."

"I already called Mrs. Pensick."

"Mary Alice's mother? You called her?" In the history of knowing my mother, I cannot recall a single time when she called anybody's mother; we were the kind of family who spent Christmas day alone. "You dialed the number and you spoke to her about me going to a sleepover party?"

"Yup."

"So I guess now I'm sort of normal. Gee," I say, smiling, "I've just turned into Barbie. This must be the Malibu Dream House. Wait—why do I see tombstones outside? Barbie doesn't have a single thing to do with tombstones. Not a thing."

"Elizah, it's not like I ask you to do a whole lot around here. But this party is not something I'm going to back down on. No negotiation on this one. This is as simple and irrefutable a request as brushing your teeth or taking a shower."

"But at least I feel better after doing those things," I say. Mom sits down across from me, holding her chin in her hand. "Do you think I will feel or act any differently after going to Mary Alice's Halloween party? Think about that, Mom. Kids in my grade are sneaking around with beer and condoms and she's having a Halloween party."

"So beer and condoms are better ideas?"

"No one is saying that. It's just, c'mon, Ma. A Halloween party?" My mother continues to gaze at me while holding her chin in her hand. I look right into her eyes. "I still can't believe you called Mary Alice's mother. I would be less surprised if you'd grown another head. Seriously. Just sprouted an entire new region of cranium with a brain and hair and articulated eyelids." I wait. My mother smiles weakly.

"I told you a lot of things would change once we moved to Wenspaugh. You have to go, Elizah. It's sort of a deal I made with Mrs. Daytner. She won't leave you alone otherwise."

"So you made a deal with Daytime for me to be social so that she will eventually leave me alone?"

"Not exactly. It's more to show Mrs. Daytner that we trust her intentions."

"We? You've never even met Daytime." I push the rest of the sandwich toward my mother. "Wait a minute. She—or you—can't make me go to a party. That's ridiculous. School can't dictate what I do on a Saturday. This is like being raised by the Taliban."

"Hmm…" My mother smiles and stands. "A little, it is. But did you ever think I don't want you to grow up like me?" She turns and walks over to the sink. I follow her.

"You're actually serious. You actually are going to make me go to a party with a girl who acts out Ukrainian folk tales at the library and organizes picnics for retarded people. You're actually doing this."

My mother doesn't turn around. "It will be good for you. Every once in a while, Elizah, it's good to leave the company of the dead."

တ

One great thing about this house, aside from its closeness to the river and its view of the mountains, is the tiny bathroom next to my closet. I can avoid my mother longer if I don't need to use the bathroom on the main floor. For now, while my mother is safely in the front office talking to the genealogists again, the sink is the perfect place to clean and examine my bone.

I slide the bone out of my pocket and begin washing it. A puddle of dirt flows from its crevices, clogging the sink with tiny rocks that I have to loosen from the bone with the edges of my comb. After I pluck out a rock the size of a pea, the bone breaks, clattering together with the delicately destructive sound of shells knocking into one another.

"Damn," I whisper, "I broke it. The perfect bone." My finger grazes a smoothly bumpy section. I stop moving. What I'm feeling is shaped like a molar. I turn the faucet up, run water furiously over the piece in my hand. It's clear now: this is a jawbone. What I felt was not shaped like a molar, it *was* a molar. And the bone is not broken. The motion of dislodging the pebble opened the hinge. What I hold in my hand on this bright October afternoon, while girls ride canoes and the genealogists map their singular histories in the front room, is the jaw of someone who died in Wenspaugh.

And I'm the only person who knows it's missing.

"Elizah," my mother calls through the door. "I thought we should make cupcakes for Mary Alice's party, and I have some ideas on what we should do. I told her mom that I would. Why don't you come look at some of the design ideas I found for Halloween cupcakes?"

"Cupcakes. Don't we have like a couple of weeks?" I

wrap the bone in paper towels and place it behind a clutter of shampoo bottles on a shelf.

"I'm not making them now, just asking you to help pick out a design."

"I don't care."

"That's not the question, Elizah. Actually, I'd like you to come out of your room now. That's really what I want."

"Cupcakes for a sleepover party," I say while walking to unlock the door. "This is a far cry from a woman who reads books on how to channel the dead."

"Yes, but just because I read about the paranormal doesn't mean I can't bake cupcakes and join the PTA."

"Oh, I don't know about that. I think it might. I think they 'out' you if you read anything other than those diet and recipe magazines that teach you how to wallpaper closets. The PTA and the paranormal don't exactly coexist." I slide the deadbolt open and follow Mom into the kitchen.

"I made lasagna for dinner."

"Great," I say, sliding into a seat. "Then we can discuss the cupcakes while we're eating. Maybe we should put the Food Network on."

"We don't have television here," Mom reminds me. "There's a word," she says while cutting the lasagna into squares. "Comorbidity. I remember it from college. Sort of sounds like what we were talking about with the PTA and the paranormal. When two states exist at the same time."

"I thought you left college when you met Dad."

"Not right away. I dropped out so he could get his

MBA. And it's not like the only thing I remember from college is your father. You want cheese grated on this?"

"No thanks." I watch my mother carefully after mentioning my father. She slices bread with no emotion on her face.

"Elizah, do the girls at school ever say anything to you about where you live? I mean, that I'm the caretaker of the cemetery or anything?"

"I try not to talk to them."

"I know. But do they ever…"

"No, Mom. Most people at school listen to their iPods or talk on their cell phones or text. It's nothing like when you went."

"I doubt that." She sprinkles grated cheese on my lasagna after I've asked her not to, and passes me the plate. "So it's not that I'm the caretaker that's keeping you from making friends?"

I shake my head.

"So do you miss your father?" She sits down on the floor, crosses her legs yoga style, and closes her eyes.

"I guess. But every time someone asks me, I feel like I'm not missing him enough or something."

My mother murmurs beneath her breath, "He skipped out on his trial, you know." She opens her eyes and lifts her palms. "So it's not just you that he left."

"Just me?" When I say this, my mother looks over at me with her palms in mid-air. "He sort of skipped out on you, too," I say.

"Yes. But what I meant was, he skipped out on everything he was supposed to do. Pay back his boss, support his family, everything, not just you. Do you remember how he left so many times when you were small?"

"Yup. Only he's not coming back anymore. Is this supposed to be an epiphany?"

"No." Mom pulls her spine up like a cat. "Elizah … why is talking to you so difficult?"

I push the grated cheese off the top of my lasagna. "Because you're not really talking to me anymore. You're mining my brain like Daytime, looking for what you think might explode next."

Mom laughs. "Oh, c'mon, Elizah. You might be right. But I ask you those questions because I'm worried about you." She arches her back. "I want you to go into the dining room and see what I did."

I drop the plate off in the sink and walk into the dining room while Mom curves her spine. I can't stand the dining room; it's dark and closed as a cave and every time I walk into its darkness, I can't breathe right. Mom has cleaned the windows; she even put little pumpkins on their sills and hung up tea towels embroidered with smiling scarecrows.

"Nice. I feel like we're turning into a television family."

"Don't go that far, Elizah. I just want our lives to be different here. Nothing notorious. And come look at the cupcake designs on the kitchen table. Those magazine pages I ripped out. Tell me which ones you like."

"Make bones. I like bones."

"No, Elizah. Which one of the choices do you like?"

"God, I don't care." I go back into the kitchen and stand behind my mother, who is now stretching her legs in the air. "But listen, Mom. What would you do if you found a bone over where you saw me crouching?"

"Probably nothing. Did you find one?"

"Maybe. But I can't tell if it's human or not."

My mother stretches one last time, then begins gathering dishes. "My guess is that it belongs to one of the wolves up in the mountains. Most likely it's not human. That's a little too strange, even for me. But if it is human, at least it's near a graveyard."

"You think Mary Alice's mom would answer that way?"

My mother laughs. "I said I wanted us to change a little. Not reinvent ourselves. So where is this bone now, that you might have found?"

"It's where it should be," I answer, innocence in my voice. "Right near the graveyard."

ဆ

The bus on Monday morning is merciless: bright sun glinting from glass to chrome and into my retinas. I take a seat in the middle of the bus because no one sits in the middle, and it sends the message that I want to be left alone. Everything in school has a meaning; it's like living with a tribe of animals who judge when and how you should be attacked by the position of your tail. Usually, the less social animals can be left alone in the middle of the bus. Unfortunately, Beth Mooney has not read up on instinctual pack behaviors. She gets on at the next stop and rockets directly toward me like a heat-seeking missile sensing the sun.

"Elizah, I can't believe it! I heard you're going to Mary Alice's party. It's unbelievably fun to plan." I look to see if Beth's tail is wagging as she stands in the aisle. "I'll bet you're excited."

I turn back to the window.

"Elizah?" Beth Mooney bounces down into the seat, next to me. "You all right?"

I nod without turning to face her.

"Are you getting a costume?" She shoves her backpack under the seat with one long arc of her foot. "I think, but I'm not positively sure, not absolutely sure, that I'm going to be an angel. First, I thought I would get one of those half-angel, half-devil outfits, but really, even my mom says a devil is a far cry from my personality."

"It depends," I say, finally turning to face her, "on how you define evil."

"What?" She looks at me with her round face and her eager brown eyes, and it occurs to me that she resembles, almost exactly, the face of a kindly rodent in a cartoon I once watched. "You know, Elizah, I just noticed your hair, and my aunt has a shop in town and you have...well, it's nice hair and all, but did you ever think of getting it layered, add a little body so it's not so flat?"

"I like flat. It matches my chest."

Beth Mooney laughs very hard at this. "You know, when I first met you in gym, I thought you were like an alien or something, the way you were so quiet and knew all the answers in science. I mean, who knows anything about rocks?"

"I like rocks. They're like the Earth's bones. And I like bones."

Beth grins. "I guess, but I mean, who really wants to know stuff about rocks? But you do. You know all this stuff. How they're made, the types. You actually said this in class, you actually spoke, and Poulle was like, oh my God, she is a-mazing. Remember?"

"Yeah. I read about rocks a lot when I was younger. That's all."

"And you were always so quiet, plus, I mean, living in a graveyard and all. I thought you were just way out there, ya' know?" She smiles. I keep looking at her. "It's not like a lot of people actually move to Wenspaugh, so after a while I realized it was probably me." She laughs again. "But I hope you think more about going to my aunt's shop. She has this whole line of new things for lifestyle makeovers. And since you just moved here, maybe you would like it." Beth holds up a purse that looks like it's made from turtle shells. "See this?" She strokes the turtle shells. "It's a cross between leather and plastic, this cool stuff that looks like leather but doesn't have to be cared for like leather. It's called pleather."

The bus lurches onto the main road near the school

and I look above Beth Mooney's head at the smooth hull of the bus. I imagine stalactites crusting over on the hull's surface, their points fanging above me and Beth.

"Anyway, I'm just so glad you're going and that you're just a smart, quiet kind of kid. I shouldn't tell you, but I'll burst if I don't: Mary Alice's mom is going to have a medium come to the party to do a séance. So spooky. I've always wanted to go to a séance. Always."

I watch the imaginary stalactite drop, piercing Beth Mooney's skull.

"Ooops, now there's a smile, Elizah. See, I knew the idea of a séance would make you smile. I could just tell."

ᔪᢍᔭ

Daytime calls me down to her office right before gym even though it's a Monday and I'm supposed to see her only on Fridays.

"Really quick today, sweetheart, since I'm running behind, but I just made a quick call to your mom and we decided it would be a good idea if you participated in some sort of community service here at school."

"Community service? You mean like building roads, like stuff they did on chain gangs?"

"No, I mean if you don't want to join any of the clubs or participate in the activities, maybe you could assist in the gym or in a classroom. I have a list of teachers who have asked for student assistants. Usually, the students pick a subject or a teacher they like. Do you have anyone in mind?"

"I guess Poulle."

"Ms. Poulle." Daytime looks down at a clipboard. "Well, you're in luck." She says this triumphantly, as if I have come to her office on my own and asked to do this and I was hoping for the opportunity. "She's on the list for Wednesday and Friday afternoons. I guess those are her lab days, huh?"

I shrug.

"I'll write you a pass to go back to gym, and you can start this Wednesday. How does that sound?"

I take the pass. "Would it make any difference if I told you how it sounded?"

∞

On Wednesday, Ms. Poulle shows me what she wants done in the room, mostly washing out beakers and making sure all the lab equipment is put back. I'm done in about ten minutes. I'm looking at the rock display when she comes over to me.

"All done?"

"Yeah."

"You get student service credit no matter how long it takes," she laughs. "There's more to do as it gets later in the semester." She looks at me for a few seconds. "I'm glad you're doing this, Elizah. I was wrong about you; I didn't take you for a student service volunteer."

"I didn't volunteer. My mother and Mrs. Daytner are making me do this."

She smiles. "Well, you put that rather directly. But that's good, Elizah. A science mind has to be direct."

I nod.

"Elizah, do you think one day I am going to figure out what you spend your time thinking about?"

"Probably not."

Ms. Poulle laughs. "You remind me of a sphinx, of a riddle I can't solve. But maybe that's why we have Mrs. Daytner; she'll figure you out."

"I doubt that," I say quietly.

∞

For the next two weeks I spend Wednesday and Friday afternoons in the science room, cleaning and organizing equipment while Ms. Poulle tells me stories about the history of Wenspaugh. Her grandmother was the town historian, so she knows all this stuff about the Indians and early settlers. I listen and look out the windows at the mountains while she talks.

"So were there a lot of wolves in the mountains?" I ask casually one afternoon. We're putting igneous rocks into the display case. "It seems like there might have been a lot."

"Wolves. I suppose there used to be quite a few more. Why? Do you like them?"

"I guess. I just think I might have seen a jawbone of a wolf by the river."

"Oh, that's right. You mentioned you like bones."

"I do."

"So did you keep it? The jawbone?"

"Nope. Just left it there."

"Oh." She turns back to the display. "If you had it, we could put it in the room, part of our mammal wall. Maybe check to see if it's still there."

"I'll check. So would you be able to tell, like, the differences between a human jaw and a wolf jaw?"

"I would hope so." She laughs. "A wolf has forty-two teeth, and a human has thirty-two. That would be my first clue. Why do you ask?"

"I wasn't sure if the jawbone was actually a wolf's. I drew a picture. Want to see it?"

"Sure."

I take the pages out of my backpack. "I had some extra time, so I sketched all the angles I saw."

She takes the sketch and looks at it closely. "Oh, Elizah, this does look like a human jaw. Look at that." Ms. Poulle studies my sketches for a few long seconds. "Very nice drawings."

"So it's human, definitely? How can you tell that, other than the teeth? Like what if the wolf lost ten teeth or something? Or maybe it's a bear jaw."

"Look." She pivots her finger against the stumps and rises on my drawing. "There are no empty sockets there to show missing teeth; there aren't forty-two spaces in this jaw. And this poor fella is missing a few here and there, mostly in the back, and the dark marks on this back tooth … I'm not sure if you just took liberties there or what."

"No," I say, following her gaze, "there were marks like that on that tooth."

"Well, I can't be certain, but to me that looks like crude dental work of some sort. Not too many animals see a dentist. But it's the number of teeth that gives it away for me. These are excellent drawings, Elizah. Are they for me?"

I hadn't thought of giving her the sketches.

"Yes," I lie. She walks over to her whiteboard and pins the drawings around the cork piping.

"There. Art in science. My grandmother told me this story once about how holding a human jaw means you own the voice of the person who once spoke on the Earth. A legend of some sort…" She squints. "Only I probably shouldn't be telling you about legends in a science classroom."

"Wait. You own the voice?"

"Well, I don't know. That's according to the legend. Actually, my grandmother told it to me. She collected legends from the Shawangunk Mountains, and was kind of an expert in folklore. I don't think many of them were written down." Ms. Poulle laughs softly. "We used to say the mountains around here gave rise to a lot of stories because of the long winters, all that sitting around at night with nothing else to do."

"Do you think any of the legends are true?"

"True? You mean provable?"

I smile. "I guess I mean, are they based on something. That's what I mean."

"Wenspaugh legends are a blend of Lenape Indian mythology mixed in with Appalachian legend and a dash of Christianity, so I'm not sure about proving anything. They're beliefs, and maybe somewhere, someone along the line saw or interpreted something that became legend. Who knows? But I do remember the jaw being significant. Finding or owning any bone that had been a body part was significant."

"Body parts? So, like, how often did people find body parts? That's sort of weird. I mean, to just come across a human bone."

"Now it is, but it wasn't then. Graves weren't all that deep, especially by the river where bodies were traditionally buried and the soil is so porous. And they didn't have hyperbarically sealed coffins like we do now. Sometimes people were buried in a simple blanket and when the spring rains came, there was a lot of flooding and the bodies loosened in their burial spots and floated. Of course even if there was decomposition, the bones would be left."

"Right. But wouldn't animals get the bones?"

Ms. Poulle shrugs. "I guess not all of them. People used to fish and hunt down by Slant River all the time so they would be able to find them not too long after they had floated back up. It happened enough that there were legends corresponding to what you owned based on which body part you might find. The jaw was for the voice, the leg bone for walking, the arm bone for carrying, and any part of the spine for standing straight. That's what I remember. Oh, and I think any part of the head, which would probably include the jaw, meant you owned the dreams, or at least some of them. After you die, the legends say, you go on a journey and you need all those body parts."

Ms. Poulle shrugs. "It was a good story when I was small. Maybe a little silly now." She turns back to her papers. "So thanks, Elizah. I appreciate the drawings. It isn't every day a student brings in portraits of a bone."

"You're welcome." I wait a few seconds.

Ms. Poulle looks at me. "What is it, Elizah?"

"If you own their voice, the person's voice, or their dreams or another one of the bones, do they come back to find whatever they are missing?"

Ms. Poulle angles her head at me in a strange way. "I thought that idea might scare you. Forgot who I was talking to for a minute."

"So they do come back? Their spirit or whatever?"

"According to the legend, if you believe in legends, yes. See, I was raised mostly by my grandparents, who had lived here their entire lives, so they knew the stories of their grandparents. I think death was accepted more easily back then, along with spirits and all. The old-timers viewed death as just a curtain your spirit stood behind. They saw ghosts everywhere, especially around the mountains and river."

"Actual ghosts? Or just like creepy stuff?"

"They believed they saw actual ghosts. They would speak with them and they weren't afraid. Or so said my grandmother. I, myself, have never met a ghost."

"That you know of."

Ms. Poulle laughs. "I suppose you're right on that. I might have met a ghost at one time or another and not realized the person was a ghost."

"Not if the dead really are part of the living, right?"

"Right. But yes, I do remember sometimes when I was small, my grandmother would say, 'Watch out for that man by the river. He's trying to find what he needs to move on in his journey,' and my sister and I would run pretty fast away from him. We knew exactly what she meant, and after we were safe up in a tree or somewhere, we would watch whoever Grandma had warned us was a ghost. Silly, I guess, but we really did believe it back then."

Ms. Poulle's classroom phone begins ringing and she turns toward it. "I wouldn't worry about any ghosts coming to bargain with you for their voice. It's just a drawing. Even a ghost wouldn't come back just for a drawing. Now if you had the actual bo..." Ms. Poulle waves her hands in the air to dismiss the idea of me having an actual bone.

I think of the bone, washed and dry, nestled in socks inside the drawer of my nightstand.

"What then?" I ask. "What if I did have the actual bone?"

Ms. Poulle puts her hand on the phone receiver. "Oh, Elizah, if you hold the actual bone, then yes, you could expect a visitation. But I wouldn't give it another thought. That's only legend, nothing scientific."

"Right, not proven."

"Or provable. Then or now." Ms. Poulle picks up the phone, and I gather beakers from the tables and begin washing them in the deep sink.

halloween

The next week, when I'm washing beakers, I look up and Daytime is standing at my shoulder.

"Did you see Ms. Poulle's pig fetus in the jar?" I ask.

"Is that an appropriate way to greet a person?" Daytime looks at me straight on with her wide, green eyes.

"I greeted you. Don't I get social points for that?" I keep washing the beakers.

"So you like it in here, in the biology lab?" She says this in the exaggerated questioning tone normally used for hearing-impaired children.

"You don't like it in here much. I can tell by your voice."

"We're not talking about me, Elizah. Are you in here right now because you want to avoid the party?" Daytime crosses her arms. She squints her eyes and I watch the skin around them pucker.

"I have no choice about the party, now do I? You and my mother arranged that one."

"Elizah, you know perfectly well you were to get on the bus after school with Beth Mooney and Mary Alice Pensick."

I put the last beaker on the table to dry. "Only if I wanted to help with the decorating. And I don't. At least I should have a choice about whether or not I want to spend time tacking up orange crepe paper."

"I'm not understanding where all this hostility is coming from, Elizah. We are here to help you."

I lift my head up and arch my eyebrows. "Are we?" I ask. "By deciding how I should spend my time? By deciding I'm not the way you want me to be so you force me into doing things I can't stand so you can tell yourself that you're helping people? Is that how you help them?"

"Elizah, this is uncalled for. There's no reason to be difficult."

"If I wasn't difficult, you wouldn't have a job."

Daytime sits down on a chair near where I'm standing by the sink. I decide to rewash each of the beakers so I don't have to look at her.

"The thing is this..." Daytime glances out the window.

I wait.

"You have some real issues that need to be dealt with, and you spend most of your time avoiding people. Why are you in here on a beautiful Friday afternoon when you could be with girls your own age who have invited you to a party with food and music and other friends?"

"Wait. You told me I had to participate more. You're the one who forces me to come here, you and my mother." Daytime nods slowly, as though she is a sage of some kind. "And I like it in here. I like science. I like body parts in jars. More than when they were on people. So you tell me I have to do community service, then you question why I'm here. Okay. I get it."

Daytime smiles. "I see your point, Elizah. But I also think you know that if you'd told Ms. Poulle you had a party to get ready for, she would have told you to go and not stay here."

"I didn't want to." I arrange all the beakers in size order.

"Elizah, do the kids ever say anything about where you live? Make jokes or anything like that?"

"They don't. And it doesn't bother me to live there any more than living next to a car wash would. It bothers other people. It actually sort of matches my personality." I pick up my backpack. "I like being alone."

"Most people don't like being alone."

"I do." Daytime watches me, her face blank as a spool. "Listen, you know how you keep asking me to figure out why I like being alone and not talking so much to the kids around me? Like what my reason is?"

"Yes?"

"Well, lately, I have this sense that my silence is preparing me for something. Only I'm the only one who will understand it when it happens. I can't explain it any more than that because that's really all I know. It's just this strange belief that came over me right as we were leaving Queensport. Then I wanted to be quiet. Just listen and not be bothered by anyone. So I could be ready."

"Ready." Daytime leans forward. "Was it a voice telling you this?"

"No. More like a dream. You know how you kind of understand things in dreams even though they aren't spoken out loud?"

"I do."

"Like that." I take two steps back and smile.

"Elizah, you haven't told me what you are being prepared for." Daytime makes a slight lurch toward me, an awkward arcing motion. I pretend not to notice.

"I don't know yet," I say. "I really don't." I turn quickly toward the door and run outside, toward home.

But I do know, in a strangely silent way. I feel that I am not alone, that in the silence, someone is coming to me, to be near me. And if I told Daytime, she would say it had something to do with my father, with missing him, or his absence.

Only I know it doesn't.

It's something new.

I stop running and walk quickly. By the time my house comes into view, light is leaving the sky. A few geese pierce the orange light, and I look into the graveyard to see a man standing in the old section on the riverbank, near where I found the bone.

The man wheels around to look at me. He has long, wild hair and clothing that flaps around him like a scarecrow.

"Almost dusk," I yell, pointing to the sign that clearly states the graveyard closes at dusk. I realize he might be too far away to hear me, so I walk over to the sign and point to the line that says the closing time.

But when I turn back, the man is gone. I look into the thickening light, but he's nowhere to be seen. He must have hidden behind the trunk of one of the wide oak trees.

"Weirdo," I mutter. For a second, I think I see him again, so I pivot quickly around. There is nothing. Just the dry scrape of leaves inside wind.

☾☾

"These are great, Elizah. So chocolate-y." Beth Mooney is biting into one of the twenty-four cupcakes my mother forced me to bring to Mary Alice's sleepover party. They have smiling pumpkins piped onto the top. We're sitting at the dining room table waiting for Madame Trusso, the psychic, to arrive. "You must have a secret ingredient in these. You have to tell us what it is!"

"Blood."

The girls laugh, but Sidra, a dark hiss of a girl, makes a face and puts hers back on the tray. She has been watching me with her teeny gray eyes ever since I got here an hour ago. I look at her, at her raindrop-sized eyes and her beakish nose. I think she is in my math class. She reminds me of something mathematical, all calculating and rigid.

"Figures you would say blood," she says. "Like, that's not even funny."

"I didn't say it was. They did." I gesture toward the other five girls, who are still laughing.

Sidra pulls her ponytail from the back to the side and begins stroking it as if it's a pelt. "So what's your story, Elizah? You don't even speak at school, and you're not saying boo here. You don't want to be here, but I can't imagine a girl like you was invited anywhere else."

No one makes a sound. Sidra and I lock eyes.

She gives a little snort before continuing. "It's not like you're emo or actually dark enough to be a Goth, so what's your story? What is it you want?"

"I want to cure blindness," I answer. "Blindness distresses me."

"Oh," Beth says, leaning over to pass Brittany a cupcake, "let's not have any fighting."

"Who's fighting?" Sidra says. "I just want to figure out what's going on with silent Elizah over there who seems so unhappy at our party. Like a dark spirit has invaded our presence."

"Well," Brittany suggests, "a dark spirit at Halloween isn't a bad thing, is it?"

Sidra arcs her brows and holds the expression while she speaks. "I've heard things about you, Elizah. All sorts of things."

Brittany and one of her clones, Miranda, start passing out cups. "So who wants juice? We also have soda. We won't be able to eat or drink anything once Madame Trusso gets here. Unless she wants to, of course. I mean, what do psychics eat? Or do they not need to eat?"

I don't drop my gaze toward Sidra. "What things have you heard?"

"Well," Sidra says, stroking her pelt-hair, "not so much about you as your dad. I heard he took money from his own company because he had this problem. Gambling, I think is what I heard." Sidra takes a cup from Brittany. "All the money from selling your house went to pay for his debt, and now he's disappeared. He's some sort of criminal. He, like, left your mother with all his debt and ... he disappeared, just like a ghost."

I sit sphinx-still for a second. "So who told you that?"

"Who didn't tell me that?" Sidra flings her pelt-hair behind her. "It's like ... on the news practically."

"Girls," Mrs. Pensick calls, "the psychic is here." She ushers in a woman wearing a flowing blue dress. Madame Trusso has wound a green scarf around her skull so only her face is visible inside the green, a small, white cloud centered in the sky. With her expanse of blue, and the white face inside the lozenge of green, Madame Trusso reminds me of one of those maps of the Earth as seen from space. She sits at the head of the table and begins placing small cones of incense in a circle.

"We are here," Madame Trusso says, "to call forth the spirits of those who are not physically with us, to bring forth the essence of those souls." She lights the incense and Mrs. Pensick dims the lights. "We want to call forth those troubled souls who still converge upon our lives without any physical presence. That is who we are summoning."

Beth pats my hand and winks.

For a minute, I do not think Madame Trusso is speaking of the dead; everything she says makes me think of my father.

⚮

That night, I wake in the fetid air of Mary Alice's basement where there are seven of us camped out like field soldiers.

While the girls sat watching a horror marathon, I had trapped spiders that crawled into Mary Alice's bathtub. I hold them now inside a plastic cup ringed with yowling ghosts. I flip the cup over, holding a wad of toilet paper over the open end. Moving with the swiftly silent motion of spreading water, I gently plunge the cup down into Sidra's sleeping bag, but not before taking the toilet paper lid off. "Happy Halloween," I whisper into Sidra's hair.

Then I let myself out, in the middle of the night, and walk the long way home. I follow a path along the river that winds around the woods and leads to the back of the graveyard. At the edge of the cemetery, just above the river, I pause as a shadow flickers past me. Chills run through me like electric current, and I stand there, waiting to see the shadow again. But it's only moonlight igniting the darkness to cobalt, and inside that light, the headstones and bushes float without edges, as if I am walking through a place that will evaporate the moment I touch it.

⚮

"We thought something terrible happened," Mary Alice says the next morning on the phone. "Like you'd been kidnapped."

"No. I just couldn't sleep," I say. For the last few minutes, I have been touching the bone, moving it around, amazed at the way it's hinged. Through my window I can see the man, the same man I saw yesterday walking in the graveyard at dusk, moving back and forth between two sections of the graveyard. He never turns to face the people visiting. I wonder if he's deaf. A boy with shoulder-length hair approaches him, and they go down toward the riverbank.

"My mom...I mean, you could have talked to me or my mom if you couldn't sleep," Mary Alice says in a breathy, beauty-contestant voice. "We would have helped you."

"Thanks," I say, "maybe I will next time. It's just really hard for me to sleep at other people's houses. Would you mind if I just went to sleep now?" I don't want to talk to her anymore because my mother has just walked into my room wearing her exasperation face. I lay the bone into its nest of tissue paper and put the lid on the box before shoving the box behind my pillows. She doesn't notice.

"What the hell was that about last night?"

"I had a great time, Mom," I answer. "Thanks for asking. They voted me most congenial. And I got a goody bag to boot. Want to see it?"

"I didn't even know you were here," she says, leaning against my doorway. "Imagine how I felt when Mrs. Pensick called this morning. How do you think that makes me look, Elizah? That I don't even know where my own child is at seven o'clock on a Saturday morning?"

"Like…how you look. Right, Mom. Never mind why I left or how I walked home in the middle of the night. Let's focus on your mother of the year nomination." I'm still dressed from the night before, so I stand and walk toward the door. "Because we have to see what's important here. I did what you wanted. I went. We never discussed how long I had to stay. So I figured the duration was up to me. My interest in staying there just sort of expired."

"Expired. Jesus, Elizah. How can you say that so callously? These people were being perfectly nice to you…"

"Right. But I didn't ask for anyone to even notice me, let alone invite me to their house. That's what you want. Not me."

"Elizah, you are grounded, hear me? Grounded. Tonight I'm having some friends over to plan a ghost-walking party, and I expect you to behave."

"So if you're grounding me, then don't dispatch me to any more dorky parties that you and Daytime cook up. I'm fine staying here. Ground me forever. That's exactly what I want anyway. Don't send me anywhere."

"I can't believe you did this," Mom says, and shakes her head back and forth.

I walk past her and out the side door. I don't look back at my mother or the house as I head down to the river. The morning buzzes hot and yellow; fragments from the conversations of people visiting the dead drift past. I stop on the rounded edge of a pathway where a large tree limb sags in the way. It belongs to one of the giant oaks, and I'm thinking it will be impossible to budge. But as I yank on the widest part, the wood yields, breaking away from the tree about five feet from the ground. Leaves skitter around me as it breaks. I roll the branch to the side of the path, and look back up to see the wound on the tree's bark. My eyes stop just beneath the scar on the wood: two initials, an *E* and a *Z*, are embedded into the bark.

This is the spot where the man was standing yesterday. I wonder if he'd been standing there carving his initials into the tree. I put my hand over the letters to see if there's any moisture, any sap on the wood to tell if the letters were impressed recently or not. The rough hew of the bark bristles against my skin, and heat rises from the wood when I press my palm into the letters. There is no moisture; the letters are as ancient as the tree. They had simply been obscured by the width of the branch.

"Oh, you got that branch already," Mom says, coming toward me. "I saw that when I got up this morning. It's getting windier. Guess a few more of these branches will be coming down."

"Look, do you see these letters?"

Mom leans closer to the trunk. "I see marks, but I can't tell if they're letters or not. Kind of like reading clouds. Maybe if I squint." She puts her hand on the tree trunk. "Kind of a *Z*, or maybe it's just sap that dripped."

"Does the wood feel warm to you?"

"Warm? No, not really. Sort of cool. Why would it feel warm? It's so shady here."

I shrug.

"Well, Elizah, I have to go help that group on the tour." Mom points to one end of the graveyard where a group of people dressed in colonial garb are walking along the cemetery pathways. About half a mile from the cemetery is Huguenot Street, a colonial settlement with original houses and furnishings that have been preserved. On weekends, people volunteer to dress up as colonists to show tourists how the early settlers once spun thread into cloth and churned butter. On certain weekends, they have Revolutionary War battle reenactments. I've already gotten used to seeing people walking around in eighteenth-century attire.

"Okay, don't wander off anywhere. I should be back in about an hour or so." I watch my mother walk beneath the trees, their trunks wide as doors. I watch her until she gets smaller and smaller and finally disappears inside the group.

I walk over to where I found the bone and push the toe of my sneaker into the dirt, but I find only dust. I look around for the man and boy I saw from my window, but they're gone.

I walk a little farther down, toward the river's edge. For a few minutes I sit and watch the river water holding the reflection of the mountains, the fire of the leaf colors on its surface. Then I sit up: I suddenly want to break the solidness of that surface.

A few old canoes lie in the brush, so I tug one onto the river and paddle mindlessly toward the bridge that connects the valley to the mountains. Every time I dip my paddle into the water, the fireglass of the surface breaks into kaleidoscopic pieces. I put my hand into the water, thinking how water reminds me of glass. A slight tug pulls my hand, and I jerk it back into the canoe, nearly tipping the boat over.

Current. I forgot about the current. The river is empty except for the colors, and a few geese trolling the banks. I thought there would be more people out today, tourists looking at the leaves, kids. But no one. Just me, paddling toward the crumbling stone bridge and the fullness of silence. I glide past an old farm with collapsing roofs on the outbuildings, and the paddocks, then rest the oar inside the hull, allowing the current to pull me toward the bridge. I lean back onto the curved, wooden stern, resting my fingers on the paddle and closing my eyes.

A loud scraping sound fills the air, and I sit up inside darkness.

"Heh."

I blink; I cannot see inside the mossy light. "Oh, I'm under the bridge," I say, looking around to see who has spoken. "Did I hit something?" I shimmy the paddle onto a rung of the ladder on the bridge's side to keep from moving.

"You hit the side of the piling there. You're all right."

My eyes adjust to the light. I'm looking at a boy who is sitting perfectly still inside a small canoe. He has brown hair to his shoulders, but the light is too dim for me to make out his features well.

"I didn't see anyone else on the river today." My voice sounds odd, as if someone behind me has spoken.

"Hard to see with your eyes shut, even for me," the boy says.

"Yeah." Two paddles rest across the seat of the boy's canoe. "So how come you're not drifting?"

He gestures toward a rope on the side of his canoe; it must be some kind of lightweight anchor holding his boat in place.

"I like it under here," he says. "I come here all the time. Under this bridge."

"I've never been here before," I say quickly. "Never." I'm shaking slightly, speaking very fast. I have no idea why I want to speak to this boy when I've been quiet around my classmates. "My mom grew up around here, though."

"Yes," the boys says. "People like to return to what they already know. It's comforting."

For a minute, it sounds as though he already knows I live here, and I'm not sure how he knows that. The river has lots of visitors up from the city on weekends.

"You live around here now?" He says this in the form of a question, but it still feels as if he knows me, or knows of me.

"Yeah, I live by the graveyard." Cars stop passing overhead; there is a second of silence. "Actually, our house is right in the graveyard. I can look out and see the graves from my window. And just in case you want to ask me," I say quickly, "no, I'm not afraid of the dead or of ghosts or anything like that. I sort of like living there."

The boy nods. "Being afraid of the dead is sort of like being afraid of the wind or the rain. The dead are natural forces."

My eyes have adjusted to the dimness and I see the boy's face now. He has dark eyes and sandy brown hair, and his eyes have a quality that reminds me of river water, the way river water holds images. Inside his eyes, I see a tiny reflection of myself.

"What's your name?" he asks.

"Elizah." I want to stay and talk to him, but I cannot think of anything to say.

"Elizah." He repeats my name, and I smile. "I'm Nathaniel." He picks up his paddle. "Elizah, can you hear them?"

"Who?"

"Oh, I guess you can't. But do you hear anything under this bridge?"

I shake my head. "Not people. Just cars. The water sloshing against the pilings a little. Who do you mean?"

"You're starting to listen," Nathaniel says, before pushing his paddle onto my canoe. "You are really starting to listen." His canoe lurches onto the river and he begins to drift away. "I'll see you next time, Elizah."

I want to say something to him, call after him, ask him questions, but it's as if I'm under a spell and cannot speak. I watch Nathaniel's canoe until he disappears around a bend.

And I am listening. I am really listening, but I hear only the swill of water running around me and the low bleating of a horn somewhere on the road.

"Get cleaned up," my mother says as I come through the door. "I can smell river on you. My friends are going to be here in just a few minutes." Mom is putting tiny dishes all over the kitchen table. She's wearing makeup and has her hair pulled up into a bun. She reminds me of a little girl on her way to a ballet recital.

"What's with the small dishes? Did you invite elves?"

"Very funny. This is finger food, Elizah. And I told you that tonight the paranormal group Ella Daytner invited me to join is coming over. To plan our first ghost walk." She turns and begins counting the chairs. "Seven," she says. "With the two sofas and seats on the island, that should do it. Now," she runs her eyes over me, "maybe you could take a quick shower and get those clothes into the machine. Mrs. Daytner's nephew is going to hang out with you during the party." She says this last sentence quickly, in the same manner a skilled nurse administers an injection.

"Wait. No. What? What did you guys plan?"

"Kyle is a perfectly nice boy. He's on the honor roll, and he plays the tuba." She taps her index finger to her watch. "Now, jump in the shower and try to look presentable."

"You've got to be kidding me, Mom. You can't be serious. My God. I'm fairly certain that arranged marriage has fallen out of use in the United States. Did we turn Mormon or something?"

Mom throws her arms up. "This is exactly the kind of hysterical response I've come to expect from you. You're going to spend a few hours with a friend's nephew at a gathering and you're using words like marriage. Elizah, you need to gain some perspective in your life."

"Right. And I need to be more social. Those are the goals. Not my goals, but *the* goals."

"Oh, Christ," Mom says. "Just go shower and try to be nice to him. Can't you? Just do this one thing. We have ten minutes before they get here."

I hear my mother's voice, high and feathery, in the next room while I'm toweling dry my hair. I hear Daytime, and the low voice of Kyle, the tuba boy. Right before going out to endure my mother's Saturday night soiree, I take the bone out of the tissue paper and the box. I rub the edges with the tips of my fingers. The bone is as solid and smooth as gold. When I touch it, I think of the boy I met in the canoe.

I think of the boy all through the evening, while my mother and her friends and the tuba boy talk to me and move around me. It's as if they're acting in a play, and I'm watching people eating and drinking and making plans for a ghost walk the following weekend. Kyle keeps looking at me with feverish eyes, and at the end of the night, when he kisses my cheek, I am waiting for the applause of my mother and Daytime.

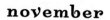
november

At first I think the papers are some sort of leftover Halloween decoration. As I walk toward my locker, I hear the papers rustle, and I see Brittany and her pack flanking my locker.

"We'll take them down," Brittany says. "We knew something…I'm really sorry, Elizah."

I look closer at the papers. They're newspaper stories taken from the Internet and printed out, all the stories from the paper back in Queensport about my father, his charges of embezzlement, about the trial he walked out on. I stand there frozen while Brittany and her clones pull the papers from my locker door. As they take them down, they glance at me. Their eyes are all sympathetic, but I see them furtively reading the printed pages. The words *fraud, family man, gambling debt, disgrace* fall on me with the silvery weight of rain, with an invisible force that holds me in that place in that hallway. I'm not sure how to make the motions to leave that spot in the hallway; the words keep falling around me.

"Elizah, I hope you know that no one here will ever hold this against you in any way," Brittany says. She whispers this while the girls around her keep tearing at the sheets. I realize pieces of the stories have been cut and pasted and made larger, almost into banners. The story my mother ran away from has been found and published and read, and will now be repeated endlessly in the hallways and classrooms of my school.

"Because, Elizah, none of us is perfect. Not one of us." Brittany says this with absolutely no conviction, in a voice that tells me she is relieved this isn't happening to her or her friends. People are walking by my locker and slowing down, in the same manner cars slow down to see if there's blood at an accident.

"Right. No one is perfect." I still haven't moved from the spot I'm standing in. My arms are at my sides, my legs clamped together in a rigid posture.

"Well," Brittany says, "we realize a lot more now. What Sidra was talking about at the party and stuff. We get it. We understand."

My backpack begins slipping from my shoulders. "What do you understand?"

"Why you're so quiet," she says. "Why you look out the window all the time and never talk about yourself."

The wolf cubs are silent. The hallway silences. All the students around my locker are looking at me as if I am going to make a proclamation. "Thanks," I murmur, though I am not at all sure what I am thanking Brittany for.

"And we'll find out who did this," one of the cubs says. "I already have some ideas."

Sidra did this. I smile at the girl, and turn away.

How could they not know that?

She went on the Internet and dug up articles from the Queensport newspaper and papered my locker with them. She wanted the girls to leave me alone once they found out details about my father and his crime.

But the girls begin making cooing sounds that remind me of doves. They rest their hands on my back and shoulder and make a protective circle around me.

"I wouldn't talk much if I were you either," Miranda says. Her hair is styled exactly like Brittany's, down to the twin bobby pins holding back her growing-out bangs. "You need to be quiet to heal from something like this."

I nod vigorously. "Yes," I say, and the girls make the cooing sound again. I move my arm to fix my sliding backpack and I smile. There's nothing I can do about my father, or about what Sidra has announced to the world, but I can work all this to my advantage.

Sidra has propelled me to victim status, granting me a perfect orbit for my silence. It's exactly what I wanted.

∞

The first period call down to Daytime's office does not surprise me. She is bristled and hackled, a wolf mother fending intruders from her brood.

"I heard," she says, "about the articles all over your locker. I'm so sorry." She just about pulls me into her office, where we sit facing one another. "So sorry, Elizah."

"It's fine," I answer. "Just fine."

"Now I think we're *really* going to have to talk about what's going on with you and your life."

I nod, remembering the narrator's voice in the wolf behavior documentary: *"Any wolf who does not conform to pack behavior is singled out by an older wolf and made to cooperate. This is done in the best interest of pack survival."*

"My life is getting better. Brittany is my new friend."

"Brittany?" Daytime gives me a quizzical glance. "Brittany Gaffin?"

"Yes, her. And I've met a boy. I'm trying to focus on the good things. There's nothing I can do about my father or the past."

She grins when I say I've met a boy. She's thinking I mean her nephew, the tuba boy.

"Yes," she says, "Kyle was quite taken by you. He says you're a very witty girl."

I smile, thinking, I don't remember anything I said to him. I was thinking about Nathaniel, the strangely hypnotic and cryptic boy, who I want to see again today.

"Getting back to what just happened to your locker, Elizah, your father never"—Daytime shakes her head back and forth—"never did he want this to happen to you. Never."

"You know my father?"

"Of course not," Daytime says, still completely justified in her assumption. "But I can tell you that no parent wants their child to go through this. No parent." She steeples her hands at her desk. "This may be a good time for you to tell me a few things about your father, about your opinion of him. And please," she smiles, "no telling me how he lives just fine like a worm."

"Right." I look at her. She smiles, waiting, expectant. I have to say something.

"Whenever you're ready, Elizah." Daytime looks down at desk, at her steepled hands.

"I don't know. I guess when I think about my dad, I just remember him coming in and out of my life, sort of like something that glittered."

"Something that glittered?"

"Yeah, like he was always so happy, so shiny-seeming compared to my mother, who I saw all the time. He would go away for long periods of time, and when he came back, he would bring me dolls or bags of candy, so he was like this here-and-there presence that I loved, but that I didn't expect all the time."

"Because he traveled so much for his company?"

"Yeah. I saw this movie in social studies about kids who eat fish, heads and all, the eyes, the scales, the whole fish. They just ate it."

"And this is connected to your father because..." Daytime shifts in her chair. She flattens her hands.

"See, the kids never had pizza or cake or ice cream. Nothing like that. So they never wanted it. They just wanted the fish and the head and the eyes and the scales. Because that's all they ever knew. When I saw that movie, I thought, that's sort of how it is with parents: you don't expect what you don't know about. My father was never around all that much, so now it's like it always has been. Except that he doesn't show up from time to time."

"But that's the problem, isn't it, Elizah?"

I shrug. "I think at some point I expected him not to show up anymore."

Someone knocks on the door and Daytime gets up and tells them to have a seat outside.

"Elizah, we need to explore this whole area of your father a bit more thoroughly, but I have to say I think you have taken this latest assault very well."

I want to ask her, what, exactly, was I supposed to do? But I just nod and smile like a dim-minded child responding to praise.

"Are you really all right after that?" Daytime asks, and before I answer, she says, "We can get to the bottom of this, you know. We can find out who did this to you. I'll ask around. I have my ways."

"It's okay," I say. "It's fine, really. Now everyone knows that my father is sort of a felon with a gambling problem. It was inevitable. Sooner or later they would find out."

"Elizah, I'm going to have to call your mother and tell her what happened. But I'm sure she's going to be mighty happy to hear that you're handling this with such maturity."

The narrative voice speaks again: *"As the wolf matures, the pack elders begin to watch the wolf with less vigilance."*

The bell rings. Daytime pulls out a pass and begins filling it out. "Can you tell me, in your own words, what you think is going on with you all of a sudden, that you are showing this level of maturity?"

I think of Nathaniel, of the strange, echoing sounds under the bridge, of the way the water sounded almost like words, of his eyes, of the warm air, and I look at Daytime.

"I think whatever my silence was preparing me for has finally begun."

"Wonderful," she says, handing me the pass. "Absolutely wonderful."

"Yes," I say, sliding out the door. "It certainly is."

That afternoon, my mother has the shades drawn against the amber light. "It's bouncing all over the place," she tells me. "I can't think straight." She holds her palms to her temples and moves them furiously to show me how her head is all scrambled. Then she goes back to cutting fruit into a bowl.

"You can't think straight because of the light?"

"I can't."

I put my books on the table and walk over to her. "So Daytime called?"

"Mrs. Daytner told me what happened, yes. But she told me some good news as well."

"About how I'm maturing?"

"That, and also that Kyle would like to take you to a basketball game Saturday. He's on the team, and the game begins around two, but since he has to warm up, you guys are going a little early. Around one, he said. Then he can come back here with Ella for the ghost walking party."

"I see. And what else has the Taliban decreed for the child bride?" I take a plate of fruit salad.

"Not to be so fresh. Anyway, I'm glad you're taking this

so well, about your father and all. Some kids would just freak out."

Freak out. I smile. Mom and her attempts.

"Not me. I rarely freak. Do you ever wonder if Dad will ever look for us?"

"All the time. Wash your hands before you eat that fruit or you'll come down with cholera from those school germs."

I look at my mother as she says "all the time," at her face, at the softness of her eyes. After all my father's done, she still loves him.

ॐ

The canoe is exactly where I left it, half hidden in the brush. For the first time since we moved here, the air is chill, veined with coldness. But the water, when I get out onto the river, is suffused with a dusty golden powder, and when I drag my finger along the water's surface, the water is warm, the temperature of blood. I'd forgotten how water holds the last season's warmth or coolness.

I paddle slowly, pretending I'm not looking for Nathaniel. Wind begins puckering the surface of the river water; leaves scud around me. I see the bridge, but there's no one there. I'm the only canoe on the river. A few geese fly overhead.

When I reach the bridge, I wedge the oar between two pilings as a kind of anchor. And I listen. I shut my eyes, but I hear only the water, the dry husking sound of leaves inside wind, the drone of cars overhead. I put my hands, palms up, on either side of the boat, remembering how my mother once took a meditation class and they told her this posture allowed thoughts and ideas to enter more easily.

I'm sitting like this when a slight pressure touches my wrist. I open my eyes. Nathaniel is smiling, his canoe partially under the bridge so half his face is lit by the setting sun; half is in shadow.

"Hey," I say. "I didn't hear you rowing."

He doesn't move his hand from my wrist; his fingers are curved over to the top part of my arm. The cool heat of his fingers reminds me of a time when my father and I were looking for bird bones in the woods. I had reached under some ferns where I saw some feathers, and through the loose weave of the ferns, sun was igniting the soil. I remembered that moment because it was so odd: coolness and heat, and being able to feel both at one time. I had not remembered the mingling of coolness and heat until Nathaniel touched me: his skin was like that soil, like the light beneath ferns.

"You're trying to listen, Elizah." He lets go of my arm.

"Still nothing. Just sounds I would expect."

He nods.

"Do you go to the school here? At Wenspaugh? I've never seen you."

Nathaniel looks upriver, back toward my house. "No. I learn at home."

"You're home-schooled?" He's still looking toward.the river.

"I have to go soon. I have to get back," he says, and pulls his oar from the piling. "You live by the cemetery, right?"

"Yes."

"Elizah, let's meet there on Saturday, all right? I have things to do before then, so let's just meet on Saturday. I'll show you where I live."

"Where exactly do you want to meet?"

Nathaniel looks up the river, and for a moment I see worry on his face. He turns back to me. "We can meet by where the river enters the cemetery, in that small space by the path. Can you come about five?"

I remember Kyle and the basketball game. "I'm not sure." Nathaniel begins to glide away from me. His hair fills with reddish highlights in the sun. It's long, unshaped, and falls to his shoulders in slight waves. "I'll try though, all right?"

"All right," Nathaniel says, without turning around to look at me again. "I'll be there at five. I'll wait for you, but I can't wait very long."

I want to paddle after him, but something stops me. As I reach for the oar, I stop mid-air; it's the voices. I hear them: low, chanting, toneless. I cannot make out words, but I recognize sounds.

"Nathaniel," I say and turn. I want to tell him that I hear them. "I just heard..."

But he's gone. The light is beginning to leave the sky so I paddle back, all the while hoping to catch up to him. But he has vanished into the gauzy air over the river.

On Saturday, at one o'clock, Kyle arrives carrying a green rectangle.

"What do you supposed he's got in that box?" my mother asks, her voice rising with excitement. She's sitting in the half-moon shape of our window seat, sifting through a box of kitchenware. I come up behind her to watch Kyle walking up the curved path up to our door. He's wearing a football jacket with the number 17 on it. "See the box?"

I nod. "I think it's a small, well-behaved squid that he's taught how to live on land. Did you know they're the largest creatures living in the ocean? Squids. Imagine snorkeling and coming across a giant squid. What would you do? You couldn't scream under there or anything. God. Imagine."

"Exactly how miserable are you going to be at this basketball game?" my mother asks. "And will you be equally miserable at the ghost walking party?"

"Nope. Just trying to get through this. I'm not exactly up on basketball strategy."

My mother holds some dented spoons up to the light. "See these? I got them at my bridal shower. Seems like a scene I watched in a movie once, now." She puts the spoons down and wipes her hands as if the memory of her shower has dirtied them. "If we want to assimilate into society and be normal, we have to learn about sports. That was a big problem your father and I always had: we didn't follow the football or the baseball stuff, and all the neighbors did. At least you'll have a fighting chance if you learn about this stuff young."

Kyle rings the doorbell. I look at my mother before grabbing my sweater. "Only if you want to assimilate. That's what you want to do. Remember, that's not any goal of mine."

ॐ

"I was thinking about you last night," Kyle says as we walk toward the high school. "For a long time." He puts his arm across my shoulder as he says this, and I think, when did I say he could do that? But I don't argue or act offish; being with Kyle makes my mother and Daytime think I'm on the right path. That's what she said this morning when she was on the phone with Daytime: "When I see Elizah with Kyle, I just know she's on the right path."

While they were talking, I was looking at the bone, moving it around, flicking tiny specks of dirt from the jaw line. With it clean like that, I could clearly make out the shape of a human jaw. As soon as my mother's voice stopped speaking, I placed the bone carefully back into the box and slipped it into my nightstand drawer.

"Oh, look." Kyle points to the colonial-simulation people. "They're going to do a musket demonstration."

"How long do they do this? Do they do it in cold weather?" We stop and watch them for a few seconds.

"They stop once it snows. But even then, they open the houses up and do demonstrations inside. They have all the original furniture."

"Huh." I look at Kyle in the cold, bright light. He has the features of a squid: small, hooded eyes, and a flat nose inside wide cheeks. That's why I thought he might be carrying one in the green box. As I'm thinking this, he leans dangerously close, and I think he's trying to kiss me.

"Kyle." I say this in the same manner that my mother says my name when I spill something.

"Sorry."

"Let's just go to the school. I'm not really big into muskets."

"Right." Kyle takes his arms from my shoulders. He's silent on the ten-minute walk to school, still holding the box beneath his arm. At the school's doorway, he hands me the box. "If you want to paint your face, I have everything you need in here."

"Paint my face?"

"Yeah. You know. Look." Kyle points to a few girls standing at the entrance of the gym. They have orange and green stripes running down their faces. "It's just to show support."

"In a war though, right?"

Kyle squints at me. "Huh?"

"Don't people paint their faces before they go into battle?"

Kyle keeps squinting at me. "I don't know if they do or not."

"Never mind." I take the box. "Is face painting required?"

"Required?" Kyle scrunches his face up. "Elizah, haven't you ever been to a school sports game before?"

"No. Never."

"Well, here." He taps the box I'm holding. "Just in case you want to support the team. Or me, you know? It would be nice."

"Right."

"I'm gonna go change. I'll see you after the game."

"Okay." I'm still standing in the same spot, holding the box, when Sidra sidles up to me.

"So, Elizah Rayne. Place a bet on the game?" She's standing with a girl who snickers. "Or don't you gamble in public? Go ahead, Elizah. Figure out the odds. You have that, you know, genetic advantage."

I walk past her, and to do this, I have to push her arm out of my way. I walk into the bleachers, following the calls of Brittany and her friend Sophie. They have their faces painted orange and green, and I sit between them, holding the box, not noticing at first that Sidra stuck a sticky note on my arm when I pushed past her. Brittany pulls it off, and we read the word JAIL GIRL together.

Brittany crumples the note up and goes back to looking at the game as if nothing has happened. It's precisely the way my mother wants to treat everything about my father: just go on as if nothing has happened.

As if we can do that.

"So how was the game?" Mom asks before I hang my coat up. She's baking a second batch of cookies for her ghost walking party; the living room is set up with chairs and small folding tables.

"I don't know. They ran around after a ball and there was a lot of shouting by the coaches. I don't think I get the whole point of it all."

"Ella tells me Kyle is some kind of basketball prodigy. They're eyeing him for a scholarship. He's very talented."

"Monkeys value that." I take a handful of cookies from the counter.

"Basketball?"

"No, the ability to throw and catch and stuff. That's how they pass coconuts and bananas from tree to tree. So how is that a talent?"

"It just is, Elizah. At least colleges see it that way. He's a very popular boy, Kyle."

"You mean in monkey culture or with me?"

My mother rubs her forehead for a few seconds. "With the kids at school, he's popular. Most boys who excel at sports are popular."

"I just don't get why throwing a ball is of any value. He's tall. Is that some kind of ability?"

"Make that your last cookie. Kyle's going to be here again at seven. What time is it now?"

"A little after five," I answer casually, hoping she has nothing planned for me so I'll be able to meet Nathaniel.

"All right, why don't you … "

"Mom, I told Kyle I'd call him, if that's okay." I pick up the cordless phone.

"Oh, I see." She slides another tray of cookies into the oven. "Be my guest."

"You have to give me a little privacy, okay?"

My mother holds her hands up in the air and steps back. "Absolutely. Far be it from me to get in your way." She grins.

"Right." I take the phone with me, switch it off, and ditch it in the laundry hamper before running to the river.

Nathaniel is not there. It's about ten minutes after five, and I wonder if I missed him. I look down the river at the water moving in slow eddies, at the clouds growing orange in the late fall light, at the space between the mountains and the sky where rays of sun spike. I touch my wrist where Nathaniel touched me, and fire pours from the spot. I put my other hand over my wrist to embrace the heat.

"What are you doing?"

"Nathaniel?" I hear his voice, but I do not see him. "Is that you?"

"You have to find me," he says quietly. "Follow the sound. You have to learn to listen."

The air around me has grown gray, the color of liquid steel. Wind starts on the river. "Say something else, Nathaniel."

He says my name. I turn around. I walk about five yards from the tree, toward the river, and for a few seconds, I'm in his arms. I feel the solidness of his chest, his arms.

Then he's gone.

"Over here," he says.

"How did you do that?"

He's standing in front of me, smiling. "Practice. Years and years of practice. I just move when you aren't looking."

"Or listening, right?"

He smiles. "We have to hurry."

"I know. My mother is having her ghost walking party tonight. I'm supposed to carry the lantern and look for the dead."

"What would you do if you found them?" Nathaniel gestures for me to follow him toward his canoe.

"Good question, considering we have two deadbolts on our front door to keep out the living."

"We have to hurry," he says, pulling the canoe from the underbrush. "I have to get back."

"My mom is going to kill me," I whisper. "We'll be coming back in the moonlight and ... "

"No," Nathaniel says sharply. "I'm not coming back with you. I have to stay with them ... I mean there, home."

"All right." I take the other oar and push off from the riverbank, into the shallow edge of the river. For a minute Nathaniel's face grows dark, as if I cannot see his features. I wonder if I should do this, accompany this curious boy down a river as darkness slips between the trees. What if he's taking me down the river to murder me? I watch him paddle, his strokes slicing the water evenly, pushing the boat down the banks. I look for the old farm, but we must have already passed it. We're getting close to the bridge; I could hoist myself onto the ladder under the bridge and scramble up onto the road.

"So," I say casually, "you aren't like planning to … murder me or anything, are you?"

"That wouldn't be possible," Nathaniel says.

"Right." His strange way of speaking again. "And why not? Anyone can murder anyone if they put their mind to it. I could murder you right now."

Nathaniel smiles and says nothing. Just before the bridge, he uses the oar to stop the canoe. He slides the oar's wide bottom through a metal ring on one of the bridge supports, and turns around so we're facing one another.

"Elizah, you can't … " Nathaniel touches my wrist again. He looks at me, his eyes soft. "We are taking a risk doing this, both of us. I don't want you to come to the village unless it's your decision, unless it's a place you want to see."

"The village? You mean in town? I've been there lots of times."

"No. This is … sort of a secret village. You have to trust me. Do you trust me, Elizah?"

Water swills around the boat; the wind stiffens, blowing my hair into my eyes. "I don't really know you that well … and … I'm not sure … "

Nathaniel circles my wrist with his hand. "I can take

you back now. Do you want to go back? I'll turn the boat to take you back home. Is that what you want?"

"No," I say softly. "I'll stay."

I look down at my wrist, and at that moment, I don't want to be anywhere except in this boat with Nathaniel.

"Then you have to listen, Elizah, and I don't mean this lightly. You can tell no one about this. No one. Ever. Not a word."

The sun is almost down over the mountains. I look at his face, then back down at his hand, at how his fingers touch the back of my hand. "So Nathaniel, what happens if I do tell someone? You sound so serious. What if I told just one person and that person swore never to tell another soul? What happens then?"

"If you do that, you will never see me again." Nathaniel strokes my skin before moving his hand from my wrist. He slides the oar out of the lock and begins to paddle again. Heat flowers where his hand had been; when his fingers ringed my wrist, I had felt only coolness. Strange, I think, how I hadn't felt the heat of his skin until he took his hand away. "If you tell anyone, everything will disappear."

His paddle splinters the water soundlessly. I watch it as it plunges into the river, but there's no sound, not even the usual gliding slip of the boat going over the water.

"You really believe you would know if I told just one person that I met you?"

"I would sense it immediately, yes."

"How?"

"You and I are inside ... it's like a circle, but you can't see it. Yet."

"You're weirder than I thought, you know that?"

I wait for him to laugh, but he says, "If you tell someone, I will feel the break in the circle, and you will never see me again."

"Right, that's how it works. The tug in the circle is the ... " I almost say *break-up*, but stop just as my lips begin to pronounce the *B*.

Nathaniel turns around and looks directly into my face. Half his face is in shadow. His left eye glitters in the light.

"All right," I say quickly. "I promise. I will tell no one about this village."

"Or about me," he says quickly. "Have you told anyone about me?"

I shake my head. "If I did, my mother would, like, lock the windows, hire a guard. Right now she thinks I'm outside talking to Kyle on the phone. It's the one thing that can get her off my back. He's not anybody, really, Kyle."

"No one can know," Nathaniel repeats. "Ever."

He turns back to paddling. I wonder why Nathaniel so often does not respond to what I say. It's worse than not listening; it's as if he hasn't heard me.

"I won't tell anyone," I say to his back. "Promise. You want me to paddle?"

"Not when we go to the village, not anymore. I have

to paddle to get there. For now, just try to forget everything you know and watch the moon."

Watch the moon. I want to shout at him, "Oh, right! Sure! That's what you say! Watch the moon! Totally normal comment, Nathaniel!" But I say nothing.

"Are you watching?" he asks.

"Um hmm." I look into the sky. The air is cold now; a chill mist rises from the river. There is only a pale dusting outlining the place where the moon should be. "It's not really in the sky so much, yet."

"Keep watching the sky," Nathaniel instructs. "Then I can paddle faster."

"You are … strange," I say quietly.

"Yes," he laughs, "I am strange. But so are you."

"I'm strange? How would me watching the moon help you paddle faster? That makes absolutely no sense at all. None."

"Sometimes you have to just let go of what you know. Just let it dissolve."

Right, I think, a little angrily, dissolve what I know and keep staring at the sky. We're inside the river's current, moving quickly past all that is familiar to me. I watch the sky and try to listen for sounds in the few minutes it takes to get to his village, but the night remains silent. Sitting in the hull of the canoe, I get the sense that Nathaniel and I are moving inside air that is inside a bell, protected by borders that I can't see.

"We're almost there. Let's pull the boat to shore."

"Nathaniel, did you notice how there was no sound on the river? Not even a bird or a rustle in the woods from squirrels. Nothing."

"It's always like that at this time."

"No, it's not. When we first moved here, my mother and I would listen to the sounds of the animals near the river at night, to the lapping water. I rememb—"

"You know how to get back?" he interrupts. "Just go left, straight down until you see—"

"I won't be able to see."

"Yes. There will be a pale light near your house."

"A pale light? From what?"

"He's ... it's always there." He maneuvers the canoe to shore, and we pull it up onto soft grass beneath a grove of pines.

"Listen." Nathaniel walks toward me and stands very close. I lean into his jacket. "The people here will not speak to you. They don't like outsiders. Pay no attention to it."

"They won't speak to me?"

He shakes his head. "We are breaking all the rules. More me than you, except..."

I put my arms around Nathaniel's waist. His arms rise around my shoulders and he holds me to him. I turn my face to his. For a second he looks down, then pulls away. "We've broken enough rules, Elizah."

"What rules?" I ask.

"I'll explain them later, or ... you will just begin to understand them on your own."

The canoe begins slipping on the flat surface of the grass. I run to get it.

"Should we tie it to something?" I can barely see now; the darkness is overtaking the light. We're standing in half light, half darkness. "Why is it slipping on smooth ground?"

"It's just a sign that we have to hurry," Nathaniel says. He stands in the same spot, making no motion toward the canoe.

"So is a canoe that slips on level grass a sign of something?"

"It moved; it didn't slip. You thought it slipped." Nathaniel smiles. "You make a lot of assumptions."

"It looked … never mind." I walk back over to him. There is only a rim of light left on the horizon.

Nathaniel touches my wrist in the same way he did the first time we met: he creates a circle with his thumb and forefinger. I stand there in the fading light barely able to breathe. "I know this must sound … impossible, but if you could just … forget what you know, what you expect to happen. What we are doing is helping someone. That's all I can say for now."

"I can do that."

"You trust me, Elizah?"

"I've come this far."

We walk for a few minutes, toward a group of houses. I have this strange sense that I'm slipping across the ground instead of making actual contact with it.

"I feel strange," I tell Nathaniel. "Really odd."

He nods and slips his hand into mine. "Once we are inside, we cannot speak. No words. Not one."

I half expected him to say that we could not speak.

"You look puzzled," he says.

"Look, this sounds totally weird, but for some reason, I sort of know what you're going to say before you say it."

He nods. "Yes, that's right. It's not surprising. Are you ready?"

"I am."

"Don't let go of my hand. No matter what."

"No words, hold your hand. Anything else?"

"No, but those two actions are very important. We have to complete this."

Complete this. No speaking. I can barely see as we step over the low, stone wall that coils around an area containing twenty or so houses, each one of them made of stone and wood and similar in design. The houses each have tilled plots in front and around the sides, but nothing grows in the beds. I look over at Nathaniel.

His face has grown dark in the moonless night; his features are no longer distinct. Even the pale chalk outline of the moon we had seen on the river has vanished. Steel blue clouds simmer in the sky, moving as if propelled by wind, yet no wind touches me.

I follow Nathaniel, and as the group of houses become clearer, I wonder if Nathaniel belongs to a cult or a sect of some kind. I'd read about groups of people who live together to support certain unconventional lifestyles; it would explain Nathaniel's home-schooling, his strange way of speaking, the rough cut of his clothing.

I stay next to Nathaniel, inside his shadow, my hand in his as we come up to the first house. I want to ask questions, to find out about him, but I know we cannot speak.

I wait.

Nathaniel stands looking straight at the house.

There is still no sound.

Finally, a woman comes to the window holding a candle. She looks out at us standing in her yard. I wonder how she can see us inside the unlit night. I look back at her, and in the dim candlelight, her eyes have the dullness of old coins. Her face looks like an outline rather than a fully featured face; it reminds me of the pale dust in the place of the moon. Her features are more suggestions of features than anything sharp and clear. It must be the candle, the way it sheds light onto her face.

She stares out at us and I see nothing behind her: no curtain, no hint of furniture or other people. I am waiting for her to make a motion toward speaking, but she stands still as stone. When she snuffs out the candle, Nathaniel and I walk in a circle around the perimeter of the house, then we move onto the next house.

A man and a woman come to the window, again holding a candle. Their eyes are dull, like shells lit by moonlight. They watch us, and behind them there is no furniture or curtains, just a window filled with blankness. We wait for them to bring a silver candle snuffer down over the flame, then we move on to the third house.

By the time we get to the fifth house, the constant pressure of Nathaniel's hand in mine, the strangely silent and shadowy people coming to the windows, the canyon of huge silence and unpierced darkness, the circles we are making around the houses, have made me dizzy. I cannot speak to Nathaniel. My body feels weighted, burdened by the air around me; all I know is the tangy smoke scent of pines, the strange circles of light, how the weight of Nathaniel's hand has begun to feel like tugging. He has not looked at me once since we had arrived in this village; he looks only at the people with an intent expression.

I begin feeling stranger as we keep walking from house to house. Ribs of panic run through me and I have to keep looking at Nathaniel's profile to keep from growing dizzier. I cannot seem to form thoughts while I stand in front of the houses, waiting for the silent presence of the people to leave.

I want to return here tomorrow, to this place where Nathaniel lives, so I try to memorize details of his village. Yet whenever I look at anything, it seems distant, as if it were captured beneath glass. The whole village seems like a mute place, a village underwater. The faces begin to run into one another, the staring seems the same, the circle we walk, the wait until the candle is extinguished ... none of it seems entirely real.

Nathaniel finally pulls me back over the wall as the moon comes out again. We run back to the shore where

I quickly slide the canoe onto the river, still lightheaded from the strange ritual we have just completed. We do not speak, but I turn to see Nathaniel standing on the river-bank until I glide past the river's first curve.

I'm glad for the moonlight; at least I can see the famil-iar outlines of houses along the river. The wind sprays river water onto my hands and face and I shiver. I know it will only take about fifteen minutes for me to return to the back of the cemetery. Just as I round the clove-shaped bend near my house, I see the old farm, lit by a sleeve of moonlight. I'm only a minute away from home now, and I look up at the hulking shape of the mountains in the night, remembering the soft weight of Nathaniel's hand in mine. I feel as if I have gone from dreaming to waking, yet I've been awake the whole time.

A loud crack startles me back to alertness. Still yards from shore, I begin paddling frantically while checking the back and sides of the canoe. Everything seems intact, but the crack has shaken the boat with such force that I almost drop the paddle. My shoulders ache with effort as I push it through the water.

When icy water soaks into my sneakers, I understand I've run into a rock just beneath the surface of the water. But I don't stop paddling to assess the gash in the boat. I move forward until I see the pale light Nathaniel spoke of. I barely get to shore before the canoe begins to list to the right and I have to jump away from it, getting wet from the thighs down. I let the canoe go into the current.

When I look up the embankment to see the light, it's gone.

The boat is gone, as if it has evaporated.

And I had not spoken to Nathaniel about when I would see him again, or what we had just done in that strange village.

Right now, Nathaniel is as gone to me as that canoe.

ℭ

"Is that you, Elizah?" my mother calls.

She's heard me sneaking through the back door into the bathroom.

"Uh, no, it's Jonas Martleby, the ghost who walks the cemetery. I've decided to take a quick shower after all these years in the afterlife."

"That was quite a long conversation you had with Kyle, wasn't it? You're going to see him in just a few minutes, you know. He's coming for the ghost walk."

"Yup. I can't hear you anymore," I holler. "The water is running too loud."

When I get back into my room, my wet clothes tossed into the washing machine, the phone on my bureau, and my mother safely in the kitchen setting up a buffet table, I sit on my bed and breathe. What would have happened if I'd split the canoe on a rock halfway home, out in the middle of the river? I can swim, but not that well, and not wearing a sweater, jeans, and sneakers. I might not have made it to shore.

"Don't you look happy," my mother says, coming into my room. "And I heard you start a load of laundry. I can't tell you how happy that makes me."

"Don't knock or anything." I'm standing in front of her wearing only a bra and pink girl boxer shorts.

"Okay, when you leave the door open, that's an invitation. But your face, Elizah." My mother comes so close I can smell the mint of her mouthwash. "You're all flushed, like you've been really happy about something very recently."

"Huh."

"I remember the first boy I had a crush on, when I was about your..."

"Ma," I interrupt, "Kyle has the personality of a light switch. I don't have a crush on him."

"Now," my mother says and sits on my bed, "what exactly is that sentence supposed to mean? He has the personality of a light switch? What do you mean by that?"

"I mean, he has two moods, and the presence of something that was created to go unnoticed throughout life. Like a light switch: on, off, there when you need it, forgettable when you don't."

"I think you're bluffing," my mother says. "I think you're just trying to keep things private about Kyle. You know, I've begun asking Ella for advice too, a bit."

"Daytime? God. About what?"

"You. How you're fresh. Your father. How he's impossible. Things like that. Anyway, I understand when you talk about your boyfriend that way; it's fine. I know you want areas where no one interferes. It's normal at this age. Ella says it's called individuation. And that's normal. Thank God we're becoming normal, Elizah."

"I don't believe in normal," I answer. "I think they made that up to make us feel bad."

"Well," she says, "why don't you finish getting dressed. I think I hear someone out on the porch."

After she leaves, I go over and take the bone from the nightstand. For some reason, when I touch it I feel closer to Nathaniel, as if he is here. I take it out of the box and hold it by the window. Maybe it reminds me of Nathaniel because it's only a small piece of a person.

And that's really all I have of him.

ℒℴ

My mother has decorated our living room so that it has this oddly festive air, sort of post-Halloween, pre-Thanksgiving. Red and blue streamers twine together around the living room beams; she's been devouring home decorating magazines and now she has a display table filled with wire birdcages and antique spoons. I look down at the display table at the same moment Kyle does.

"Sort of like an insane person's garage sale," I whisper. "Articles from the asylum."

"I like it," Kyle says, a little defensively. "It's arty."

"Hmm, I guess. It's not like there are rules for decorating a ghost walk."

"Want to sit on the couch?" Kyle says.

I make an awkward sound when he asks this, something like a sheep's bleat.

"Are you okay?"

"I think I better keep standing," I say. "I need to be ready to help Mom out."

"Oh. Right." Kyle shuffles his feet, and for a moment I almost wish I liked him. "I think I'll get something to eat. Be right back."

"I'm not going anywhere," I say.

There are about ten people in the room, more people than we had over at any one time when we lived in Queensport. My mother is going from person to person, handing out cups of punch and smiling.

She stops and talks to a man who has the kind of unkempt look of a genius: stormy caterpillar-sized eyebrows, rumpled shirt, hair that moves like sagebrush as he speaks.

"There are no guarantees," I hear him saying. "Spirits are not at all predictable. They aren't weather."

Mom is nodding vigorously, so he must be the psychic. He blinks and looks around at the party guests as though he can't quite place any of us.

Daytime separates from the guest constellation like a rogue star. She walks over to me, holding a bowl of mushroom soup.

"Hello, Elizah. Did I introduce you to Dirk yet?"

Like I'd forget meeting someone. Especially someone with a name that rhymes with jerk.

I take the soup and shake my head no.

"He's right there, heading over to talk to your mom."

"Okay." There are about seven adults here that I've never met, so I wait to see why Dirk is so important.

"Dirk's a guidance counselor I worked with over the summer. He's a really nice man. Not my type, but nice."

I look over to see Dirk leaning close to my mother. He has chiseled features and sculpted hair that rises from his forehead, so the total effect is that he resembles one of the heads on Mount Rushmore. "Oh, yeah. I see him."

"Well, you know, your mom can't be alone forever. She's still an attractive woman." Daytime smiles, and walks over to the couch where she begins speaking to the supposed psychic who's leading the ghost walk.

I sit at the small buffet table trying to process what Daytime has just said. It seems vaguely illegal that my mother is standing right in our house, talking to Mount Rushmore when she's still married to my father. But of course, my father sort of gave us away.

"We are ready," the psychic says, "to begin." The room silences. "The light of ghosts," he continues, "cannot be underestimated." He holds up an apparatus that looks like an electronic lantern. "I am going to ask those of you who do not believe in ghosts to stay behind during the ghost walk."

No one moves. "There is a certain energy we all bring to a place, and if your energy is negative, I am going to ask you to wait here. Only those who believe in life after life can come with me. I need to make that absolutely clear."

I'm still sitting at the buffet table when Kyle slides up next to me and tries to take my hand. I pick up my spoon and balance the bowl in my other hand to avoid his touch.

"Are you sure about this?" Kyle whispers. "Because I'm sort of a ghost agnostic."

"Yeah, I guess. Ghosts don't bother me either way."

Everyone is putting hats and coats on, so I put the soup bowl in the sink and swipe a pair of my mother's gloves from the pocket of her jacket. I don't want the touch of Kyle's skin on my hand after having seen Nathaniel so recently. I'm zipping my parka when Mount Rushmore comes over to me.

"You're Elizah," he says. "I'm Dirk." I shake the hand he extends. "Ella tells me you're one of the kids she sees."

"Actually," I say, backing away from him, "it's more like a hostage situation. Mom forces me to go, and I don't complain because it's a way to get out of my classes. I stay the required forty-two minutes."

"So that's the hostage part, the forty-two minutes?"

"Feels like it."

"Well," he says and smiles, "that's a cool way to look at it."

Cool. The same attempts with language that Mom makes. I smile back.

"I'll see you outside," Dirk says as Kyle calls my name. Then he winks.

I can't imagine my mother spending time with him if she wasn't being given a salary of some sort.

The psychic, whose wild hair billows in the wind like a cartoon depiction of a scientist, is explaining how his gaussmeter works. "A gaussmeter measures the polarity and strength of magnetism," he says. "If the readings change, there's a good chance there's a presence here. Dirk will be holding the video camera." He fiddles with dials and gauges while the group murmurs.

"I'm going to ask you not to speak during this walk," the psychic says, "as we will be measuring voices. It's called electronic voice perception, and we can listen to it once we're back in the house. But please, no talking. This is a silent walk. I'll answer questions when we return indoors."

Dirk walks next to the psychic, holding the camera, and Kyle walks so close to me that I can feel the heat and moisture of his breath. The moon is out, bright and unshadowed as an open palm; embers of its cold light skitter down the tree branches. We walk to the eastern edge of the cemetery and the lapping of the river is audible. Everything on the walk reminds me of the village I visited with Nathaniel, the secret village that I can speak about only with him. Looking around at the group, I think how it would never be possible to have Nathaniel here with me, in the way Kyle could always be here, and I cannot say why. I know so little about him. I don't even know when I might see him again.

Kyle tugs on my elbow. While thinking about Nathaniel, I'd begun walking toward the edge of the river, away from the group. "What are you doing?" he asks.

"Sorry." I run back to the group, trying to avoid the weighted stare of my mother and Daytime.

I don't want to tell anyone that it was as if Nathaniel had been calling me to him, there by the river's edge. In the silence of that night, it was the only sound I could hear.

ℭ

"My aunt is wild about all this stuff," Kyle tells me. We're back in the living room, sitting on the couch. "She's always reading stories of near-death experiences and the afterlife and all. I think after you die, you just go into a long black sleep. Oblivion. A kind of peacelike sleep."

"Huh, sort of like pulling a hood over your eyes?" I put some tortilla chips into a bowl so my hands are busy in case Kyle wants to touch me again. Just as I complete my defensive measures, his arm circles my shoulders. It stays there, a shawl made of concrete.

"Sort of like that, I guess. I just don't think you come back. I mean, if you did, we would have some kind of proof." His body inches toward me, and I remember being little and watching worms move across rocks in the garden. My father had explained to me how certain creatures move without bones. Kyle moved on that couch with the exact glide of that long-ago worm.

"Maybe we just don't know how to prove it yet. I don't know. It's weird to think ghosts can, like, see us."

"Nah. They don't exist. With everything they have now with technology, we would know." Kyle says this matter-of-factly, as if he is quoting facts about the atmospheric gases of Saturn.

"You think we know how to look? My dad told me his grandmother said there are ghosts around us all the time, but only certain people can see them. It's a gift."

He moves his shoulder so it's touching mine. "No way. Even when people have a near-death experience, they say it's just, like, the brain emptying and sending out random sparks that we read as images. It's just black and blank after you die."

"You don't know that, though." His shoulder kind of bangs into mine and his hand is over my bra strap. I look around, but the adults are all buzzing around each other.

"I know. I just know. We would have proof by now."

"I don't know, Kyle. I think what my great-grandmother believed might be true. She said it was a gift of sight, and I guess she had it. Or people said she did."

"Sorry. Lot of hogwash, Elizah. You shouldn't talk that way."

"I think I should, at a ghost walking party after Halloween. If I can't now, when can I?"

Kyle smiles and his mouth moves toward mine.

The psychic rescues me. I turn my head as he speaks.

"You know, there's an interesting finding on the electronic voice tape," he says. "I can't be sure yet." He looks directly at me. "I have to go home to be certain, but I think I can make out one voice on this tape. It's saying the same word over and over."

I look quickly at Kyle, who is smirking. "You mean," he says, "you actually got a voice on that tape? Are you sure it's not one of us whispering? Or an old hoot owl?"

"Quite sure." The man doesn't look at Kyle as he says this. "It's fairly unclear, but I do believe it's the same word over and over."

"That's great," I say, feeling kind of sorry for this wild-haired man standing in front of the smirking Kyle. "The walk proved something, then."

The psychic shakes his head. "You don't understand. The voice is muted, but it sounds like it's saying your name over and over."

"My name?"

"Yes, Elizah. He, or she, or it, is saying it over and over. Listen." He hands me the headphones connected to the tape recorder and switches it on.

I hear static, then a creaking sound, not a voice.

I shut my eyes. The creaks come together and the voice is clearly saying my name. Only it doesn't sound like a voice: it sounds like wind rasping through branches. But the sounds it makes are unmistakable.

"Eeee…li…Eee…li…zah."

I shut my eyes. There's something about the voice that comforts me. When I open my eyes, the adults in the room have gathered around me, their faces shiny with anticipation.

"It really sounds more like a rasping sound than actual language. Almost like a scratching sound," I offer.

"That's not the point," my mother says. "Why is it saying your name?"

"It's an old name," I say quietly.

"I'm sure," Kyle says, standing to face the group, "that we're interpreting some animal sound as her name. Because rather than it being a ghost or a spirit or whatever saying something in our language, the scratching Elizah hears is probably just a tree branch or the old boats down by the river creaking. Those canoes should all be burned for termites." Kyle laughs, but the group remains silent.

"I don't think," I say, handing the equipment back to the psychic, "that we can tell either way. And I doubt we'll find out tonight."

People nod.

"She's right," Daytime says.

Dirk comes over and pats me on the shoulder as if I were a horse that had just won the race. "Nice job," he murmurs illogically. What had I done, exactly?

Sweaters and jackets appear; people begin hugging. I'm glad they're leaving. It's late, and I want to lie in my room and breathe the darkness.

ॐ

At 3:15 in the morning, my palm cradling the bone in my sleep, I wake to tapping sounds on the glass of my window. It is distinct, a code: three taps, two taps, silence, three taps, two taps. I put the bone inside the box and go to the window, my heart thrumming in my chest. Slowly, I inch back the curtain and slide the window up.

I look outside. Nothing. No branches, no strange mists of ghost swirling. The graveyard is entirely dark.

"Elizah! Down here!"

"Nathaniel?"

There, holding a small light at the end of a key chain to his chin to illuminate his face, is my father. He's grown a beard and he's wearing a knit cap pulled below his eyebrows. He's also awkwardly holding a very long stick.

"What did you say before? Are you meeting boys this way?"

"No," I answer, trying not to laugh at his parenting attempt. "I just sneak over to the window to meet fugitive parents."

My dad motions for me to go downstairs and let him in. He silently follows me back to my room and closes the door.

"Listen, kid, I'm really sorry."

"Right. Maybe you want to see Mom?"

He looks around. "I knew you'd choose a corner room. But what a creepy house. Christ. Aren't you scared in here? It looks like about three hundred people have lived in this room before."

I sit on my bed and look at my father, in his cap, with gray patches in his beard, holding a duffel bag. "It's the best Mom could do. You know. Due to her circumstances."

He comes over to the bed and embraces me in an awkward way that reminds me of holding still for an X-ray. I don't breathe in or out.

"I can't stay."

"No?"

"Elizah, listen. You can't tell anyone I was here. Not a soul. I'm going in to see Mom, then I'm out of here."

"Okay."

"Are you all right, Elizah?"

"I'm good, Dad. I'll see you … soon?"

"Not sure when. But you will definitely see me."

I go over to the window. I stay there for a few minutes, because seeing my father has made me cry. My mother is making coffee in the kitchen. I can smell the coffee, hear the hum of low voices. I'm still sitting by the open window when my mother opens the door to my room.

"Elizah, it's freezing out there," she says, pulling her robe around her thin ribs. "Shut the window. I have the heat on tonight."

"Did Dad leave?"

"He's gone." My mother comes over and sits on my bed. "I got a letter forwarded here about two weeks ago, and I wrote back and gave him our new address. He's been out in the country, doing handyman work for some old woman who lives alone."

"You believe that? Dad? Out in the countryside with some old woman? She's probably about thirty-two and an heiress."

My mother rubs her palms together and her face goes distant. "It doesn't matter what I believe. He's thinking of going back to Queensport and..."

"Going to jail?" I shut the window. "He'll never do that."

"I said thinking, Elizah, thinking. He's most likely going south, down to Florida, then over to Mexico."

"Great. Will we ever see him again?"

My mother doesn't answer me. She goes into her room and, without looking, I know she is crying.

ೞಌ

"So," Daytime says, "that was a great party your mother had over the weekend, don't you think?"

"I guess."

We're sitting in her office on a Tuesday afternoon. She told me she's having a root canal on Friday so we have to meet today. I sit and listen to her explaining a root canal without hearing the words. Outside the sky is the gray and empty, the color of seed.

"Well, Elizah, your mother told me it might be important to talk after the weekend."

"Did she say why?"

"No. I think that's up to you." Daytime winks. The skin around her eyelid gets all crinkly when she winks.

"Huh." My mother, I think, trying to do the straight thing from such a crooked place. Go talk to the counselor about seeing your father in the middle of the night when you can't tell anyone you saw your father in the middle of the night.

"Sweetie," Daytime croons, "tell me, is this about a boy? Because if it is, I have to tell you that Kyle thinks you are just about the icing on the cake."

"Oh."

"Oh?" Daytime grins. "Is that all you have to say? Oh? You know, there are a lot of girls who would love to go out with a basketball star like Kyle. Believe you me, lots of girls. And you're the only one he pays any attention to. So, Elizah, I think that's really making progress."

"I ... I don't get it. How is that making progress?" I touch the spot on my wrist where Nathaniel last touched me. I rub my skin, trying to remember what his skin felt like, the warmth and the coolness coming together.

"When you first came here, you were so alone. And now you're going out with a star basketball player and getting invited to parties. I think after Christmas, we can discontinue our sessions."

I look at Daytime. I look past her to the gray sky. I don't tell her that I have no interest in her nephew, in his face that reminds me of a face painted on a balloon, in his words that are as predictable as the words of a television game-show host. I don't tell her that I wait for parties to be over. And I don't tell her that my father slipped into my room on the night of the ghost-walking party like a ghost showing himself one last time before sliding into oblivion.

"Yes." I smile. "I think I'm making progress, too."

Three days pass before I see Nathaniel again. Wind blows through the cemetery and shakes the house; leaves have fallen from the trees. Through the bare branches, I can now see the river from our house. The water is gunmetal gray, and cold. Each afternoon, I put on a parka, zip a jacket over it, and wait on the rocks by the river's edge to see him.

That afternoon, a Friday, he comes up behind me and slides his arms around my shoulders. I close my eyes.

"Elizah."

All the things I wanted to say to him vanish.

I put my hands on his. The coolness of his skin surprises me. "You need gloves."

"How have you been?"

"Nathaniel, I never know when I'm going to see you again. Or anything about you, really."

He drops his arms from my shoulders. "You know what you need to know, Elizah."

"Yes." I laugh. "I know that you speak like … I don't know, some kind of oracle. It's unnerving."

"Do you want to leave? Or me to leave?" He's standing in front of me, his eyes golden in the late-afternoon light.

"No." I feel the strange sensation, like entering a trance, overtake me.

"I need to ask you a question," he says, touching my hair.

"Yes?"

"Do you ever find things outside?"

"Not really. Wrappers, old coffee cups, things like that."

He moves strands of my hair behind my shoulders. "Only those things?"

"Yes. Why? Did you lose something?"

"I didn't." He laughs. "You need to think about that, about my question. Now, would you like to go on the river? We can go back to my village."

"It's freezing," I say, but of course I want to go. "I touched the water two days ago and it was colder than stone."

"So you want to stay, Elizah? Here, on the land?"

"On the land. See what I mean? You have such a weird way of putting things."

"Well, to get to the village, we have to go by the river."

Wind starts again. I tug my parka over my head and Nathaniel puts his hands on my cheeks.

"Your hands are so cold."

"I'm fine. I have a boat," Nathaniel says.

"So we can't walk? Like ever?"

He shakes his head. "They are not usual, the people I live with. They can only be approached by water."

"Or what?" I smile. "What happens if we walk through the woods and surprise them?"

"They would hide, Elizah, you know that."

"Do I? How would they hide? And where would they put their houses and their yards and all?"

Nathaniel begins walking backwards. He takes three

steps. "You need to trust me," he says. "I can't tell you everything right now."

"I do trust you. But you can't explain to me why we can't just walk to your house? It's just odd, is all."

Nathaniel takes more steps, and I know that he'll leave if I don't say something.

"I'll go," I say quickly. "In your boat."

"You don't understand why we have to follow the river, do you?"

I shake my head. "I don't."

"I can't tell you."

"Is it, like, a custom?"

Nathaniel says nothing. He takes slow steps back to where he was standing before.

"Nathaniel, are your parents those people who do the colonial simulations? Is that it? I know some of them live like colonial people a lot of the time and they do research and stuff. So do you guys live that way for research or something?"

"They are there because they need to be there, and they do what they do because it is necessary."

"I give up. You know what? When you talk, all I can think of are those sayings on Chinese fortune cookies, like the ones that say *Much love is greater than much soup*. They make a crazy kind of sense, but only if you sort of add to them. You know what I mean?"

Nathaniel holds out his hand and grins. I don't know whether he's smiling because he thinks what I said about the fortune cookies is funny or because I'm agreeing to go with him on a cold river in a boat I don't see.

I take his hand. The coldness of his skin no longer surprises me.

"I have a new boat. It's important that you ride in it with me."

"Important? Why?"

"You ask so many questions for someone with so few answers," he says. His eyes glitter as he says this.

"Are you mad about something?"

"Another question," he points out, but his eyes are no longer angry.

"Right. I'll just follow along dumbly and I won't ask much. That should last about a minute and a half." I say this, yet I follow him along the river's edge to the canoe. It's mahogany colored, with brass designs on the sides. I touch the smooth wood.

"Wow. I've never seen a canoe like this before. It looks sort of . . . old."

"It is old. So just how many canoes have you seen before?"

"Not so many, I guess. This is just so different looking."

"You want to get in just as I bring it near the water. So you don't get wet."

We pull the boat to the water's edge. "It's incredibly heavy," I tell him. "Are you sure this thing floats?"

"Yes. I've done this many, many times."

We clamber into the rectangular boat and it descends

into the water's surface, but remains afloat. For a moment, when it first sinks down, it seems so heavy that I imagine it dropping all the way to the bottom of the river.

As we glide past the riverbanks, I look at the width of Nathaniel's back, at the uneven cut of his shirt, at his hair that shines even in the dull light.

"You're quiet now," he says.

"I feel a little strange, being out on the river like this. I usually think of being in a boat as a summer thing, you know? With the leaves down and stuff, it's just sort of…"

"I am always in the boat."

"There you go again, Nathaniel. Talking like a fortune cookie."

"I'm telling you the truth. The people in my village trust you now. They feel they know you."

I sit up a little straighter. "Now how is that? They just stared at me while holding candles. I don't get it. Usually you have to talk to people before they decide to trust you."

He shrugs. "That's how they are. They recognize you."

"Recognize me? I've been there once."

"It's more like recognizing your soul."

"Oh." I laugh. "Soul recognition. Now I understand completely what you mean. That's how we say hello to people in the supermarket, right? Through soul recognition?"

Nathaniel moves the paddle and says nothing.

"So, Nathaniel, can we talk while we're there, this time?"

"Yes, we can. But we are going only to my house, not to anyone else's house." He points. "From here you can see my village. Look up. See the house that's slightly higher on the knoll?"

I look and see a house, almost identical to the others, on the hill. A man sits on a log outside the house. He stares straight at us without smiling.

"He looks friendly," I say. I look at him more closely. "You know, I think I've seen him before. He was walking in the graveyard. Do you know him?"

"Yes. I know him."

"Were you with him one morning? I looked out my window and I thought I saw you speaking to him. I'm wondering if it's the same man. Is that him?"

"It could be him, but he won't be there when we get there."

"How do you know that, Nathaniel?"

"There you go again with your questions."

"Right." I shift on the canoe seat. "I think it's probably okay to ask you how you know that. I mean, like, does he have to go to work tonight, or to a meeting? Exactly how do you know he won't be there? I just wonder, that's all."

"Why does that make a difference, how I know things? Do you think it will change anything that is going to happen? If you knew what was going to happen to you in five minutes or in seventeen years, it wouldn't change the outcome, would it?"

"It doesn't in science. But it gives you an idea of what to expect. I guess that's what I'm missing with you: what to expect."

Nathaniel reaches for a rope I hadn't noticed before; it's tied to the side of a rock. He pulls on the rope to glide us closer to shore.

"No one knows what to expect, Elizah. Never. They only think they do. It brings them comfort, to plan, to expect certain outcomes."

The canoe's hull grates against the river's bottom as we enter the shallow water near the edge of the village.

"Plans are a little weird, I guess. My dad always said the lure of gambling was that nothing is ever planned. That's what makes it so exciting. 'Planned' is like...I dunno...school or a music lesson or something."

"Even planned things can surprise you," Nathaniel says. He plunges the paddle into the shallow water to stop the canoe, then steps into the dark water to pull the boat to shore. I step out.

The wind has stopped, but the sky over his village seems blacker than the sky over the river. "It's so dark here, like it's never really daytime."

Nathaniel doesn't seem to hear me. He ties the boat to a tree while I stand on the shore and look up the knoll. The man still sits on the log, as if he is waiting for us. I turn back toward the river. Suddenly I want to be home, in my room, with my mother doing the dishes while the tree branches tap against the windows. The whole trip in this strangely shaped and weighted canoe seems slightly sinister.

"What's wrong, Elizah?"

"I don't...you know, I've changed my mind. I just got, like, the heebie-jeebies or something. I really don't want to go up there right now, to the village. It was creepy last time."

A glare of anger ignites Nathaniel's face. I back away. It's the same expression he had back by the cemetery when he told me I asked too many questions.

"Elizah. Don't."

"Don't what? I'm worried that you're in some cult or something. I'm scared, Nathaniel. I don't want to go up there and be like a ritual murder victim or something. And you seem sort of angry today."

"What? I'm not angry. Elizah, I would never hurt you. No one from the village would ever hurt you. Ever. You should know that already."

"Right. Because I have so few answers, isn't that right? I have so few answers that maybe I should just go back home and not ask questions because then I could figure stuff out. And if I could figure stuff out, then you wouldn't be in charge all the time."

Nathaniel walks over to a large rock and sits down. He holds his arms out to me. "I will tell you some things," he says. "But you cannot say them to anyone."

I walk over to him, lean over, and press my face to his.

"I am far from in charge. You're the one in charge of

everything, Elizah," he says quietly. "Everything is up to you. It always has been. I thought you knew that."

He turns his head and kisses me. His lips have the same coolness as his skin, and when he pulls away, warmth spreads across my mouth. I expect his touch to be this way, now—coolness followed by warmth, the opposite of any other time someone has touched me.

"I feel sometimes…" I sit next to him on the rock. "I don't know, Nathaniel. I just feel like you think I know things that I don't know. Like I'm in charge somehow, only I can't name what I'm in charge of or why. And I go with you, and I do these things, which is so not like me normally, and then I think, what am I doing? I don't even know your last name."

He laughs. "Loomis," he says. "Now, how does that make any difference in anything?"

"It…I guess it doesn't."

"I can take you back home if that is what you want. I can't force you to do anything. Everything has to be done of your free will."

"Or else what happens? What the hell does that mean, 'Everything has to be done of your free will'?" I pull away from him and look up the hill. The man is gone. "You make it sound as if I'm in some kind of ritual all the time, and that's what scares me."

"It's not a ritual," he says quietly. "I just believe that we were meant to meet, Elizah."

He stands. For a minute I feel lightheaded, dizzy, as if

I'm standing near him and there is a cold fog all around us. But the air is light, clear as water in a glass.

"Are you going to leave and go back, or come with me, Elizah?" Nathaniel holds his hand out to me.

I take it. I put my hand inside his and wait for the coolness to spread across my skin, knowing the warmth will return when I take my hand away.

"It will be dark tonight. Can you walk home?"

"I thought I couldn't take the road from here."

"Just not to get here; you can take the road back to your house."

I nod.

"We are going to my house, just for a short time."

"Why? Is that part of the plan?"

"It is, yes." Nathaniel laughs. "Actually, Elizah, I just thought you might want to know where I live. Maybe see it."

A child moves across our path as we walk. I smile at him. He's wearing the same rough-cut clothing that Nathaniel wears, the seams uneven, the material filled with obvious stitching. The child keeps looking at me; his eyes shine through darkness, the way minerals shine. He doesn't smile or react to me in any way. He is holding a stick, and when he sees me, he takes his stick and begins drawing circle after circle in the dirt.

"Are all the kids around here so sociable?"

"He's just a little scared of you. He thinks you're a ghost."

"Me? Right, my tan has faded. Big time."

"This is my house, Elizah."

I say nothing. The house is small and square with a scatter of plant husks outside its walls.

"Let's go in. But we have to keep this front door unlatched." Nathaniel wedges a rock to prop the heavy, wooden door open.

"Why? What happens if we shut it? "

"I don't have a key. That's all."

"It's freezing in here, and it's so dark. Where's the light switch?"

"Elizah, we don't live like that."

"Right."

"Why don't you sit at the table? I'll make a fire and get some candles."

The light is dusky; I can barely make out the edges of furniture as I walk to the table. Nathaniel quickly locates candles and matches, and slowly, as if I'm watching the scene through a camera, each area of the house becomes visible. There is the large room with the table, where I am seated. A crude kitchen is behind me, with plates and pewterware displayed on shelves. Above us is an open loft where I can see three beds and a few chairs.

"No one is home, Nathaniel?"

"We are," he answers.

"It's nice here," I say. Through the window I can see the river, the last smolders of light rubbing the sky.

"You think it's nice?"

"I do."

The fire does not seem to give any warmth to the room. I wait while Nathaniel lights seven candles and places them at the table. I watch him through a large mirror hung directly behind him, on the wall to the left of the table.

"I'm watching you through that mirror," I say as he puts the seventh candle in front of me.

He turns toward the mirror, and for a few seconds, our faces are together inside the frame. Nathaniel turns back to me, and when I look at the mirror again, his face is still reflected on the glass.

"Wait. What?" I stand up and look into Nathaniel's face, then into the mirror. His face is still there. "Your face…" As I say the two words, the image vanishes. Nathaniel deftly moves away from the mirror's reach. "So how does your face linger in the mirror, Nathaniel? Is this a normal house?"

"I think it's normal." Nathaniel gestures at the leaden November sky outside. "It's just that time of evening, that time of year. Your eyes play tricks on you. You're nervous tonight, Elizah."

"Uh, no. I was looking straight into that mirror and your face was about three feet from mine and it was also in that mirror. How is that possible, Nathaniel?"

"It's not, Elizah. You know it's not."

"But I know what I saw. And I saw your face there."

"It's the light, Elizah. What you're saying cannot happen."

I look at the mirror again. "Maybe you're right." A tiny chain hangs from the mirror. I walk over and touch it. The chain has a small, golden rose dangling at its end.

"This is so delicate," I whisper. "It's beautiful."

"You found it again," Nathaniel says quietly.

"Again? What do you mean?"

"That … it belonged to my mother. She gave it to me to give to someone."

"So it's not your mother's anymore?"

Nathaniel smiles. "It was a long time ago, but I gave it to a girl. The girl lost it, but now the necklace is back here."

"Doesn't your mother want it back?"

"She wants the girl to have it. It's been in my family for a very long time, but it's been lost for even longer. The girl probably doesn't remember she left it here. I think my mother put it there so the girl would find it again."

"So the girl lives here?"

"She used to," Nathaniel says. "But she moved. Like you did, Elizah." He lifts the necklace from the mirror's edge.

"I would like you to put it on. Just once, all right?"

I slip my jacket off, and Nathaniel slowly lifts my hair from my neck and places it over my left shoulder. After he clasps the chain, I turn to him. He puts both his arms around me.

"Look in the mirror again, Elizah. See how beautiful everything looks."

Nathaniel is right; with the fire behind us, our faces look as if they are in a painting, softly lit and golden. Nathaniel kisses me on the neck, on the mouth.

"You better put this back," I say, lifting the necklace. "Your mother will be happy you found it."

"No," he says, "it's no longer hers."

I say nothing, unsure if Nathaniel is offering me the necklace. Then he unclasps it and places it back on the mirror. We look into the mirror, at ourselves, again.

"We only have a few minutes left here," he says. We both look out the window toward the river. "Then we have to leave."

"Right. Listen, I should probably get back now anyway. My mother is probably wondering where I am and all."

Nathaniel gets a candle from the table and holds it to our faces. In the candlelight, our faces look distorted in the mirror, ghostly and malleable as vapor. I watch as he pulls away; his image disappears this time.

Still, I'm certain his face lingered there the first time.

"You better get back," he says.

When we say goodbye, we kiss once more and then I run toward the road beneath the long shadows cast by the pines. Snow is falling now, faster and faster, spinning down from the sky in a way that makes the air impossible to see. I finally reach the road, and it is already covered with white. When I look back, the woods are dark; the only light that falls is from the glimmering snow.

until thanksgiving

A week later, my mother is snapping commands at me while getting ready for her pre-Thanksgiving buffet. "Elizah," she calls, her voice electric with exasperation. "How many times have I told you that we put the silverware on the side table and the plates and bowls on the main table? Nine? Ten?"

I switch the utensils with the stoneware and look directly at my mother. "I'll be back in a little while. I've been inside all day."

"Just be back before everyone gets here," she says. She does not even look up from the table when she says this.

I go down to the river, knowing I probably won't see Nathaniel, but hoping he might show up. The pewter sky matches the silver shade of the water and I sit on the large rock, gazing at the empty river. Only a few birds interrupt the silence.

I decide to take one of the canoes downriver. The current moves rapidly and it's harder to maneuver; the water is thick with cold. I try to remember the spot where we stopped the canoe at Nathaniel's village, but nothing looks familiar. I finally pull to shore at the edge of the Huguenot Street village.

I walk around the colonial settlement a few times, peering into the old wells and looking inside houses at the furnishings, at the simple tables made from planks, at beams that are polished to amber. The afternoon is lightless enough that I can see my reflection in the windows.

I'm watching my reflection appear and disappear inside the glass panes when a voice breaks the silence.

"Yoo-hoo, Elizah, over here!"

I look to the right as a car approaches. It's Daytime. I walk to the edge of the lawn, near the road.

"Why are you walking in this desolate part of town? You're so far from anything. Elizah," Daytime says, "your mother has been worried to death about you."

"Sorry. I must have lost track of time."

"Well, she's beside herself. You weren't in the cemetery and you weren't in your room, so she called me. What are you doing down here?" She opens the car door and I step inside. "I'll give you a ride back to the house."

As we drive past the woods, I peer into the trees to see if Nathaniel might be there.

"Did you lose something in the woods?" Daytime asks. "You're looking so intently at those trees."

"No, I didn't lose anything." I think of Nathaniel's face when he was asking me if I ever found things. He looked so hopeful, as if he had lost something. I would have to ask him about it the next time I saw him. Only I had no idea when that might be.

"You know, Elizah, you can tell me anything. Anything. Really. That's my job as a counselor. I've worked with young people for a very long time and very little surprises me." She glances at me for a second. I listen to the low drone of the car heater, to the wind outside the car.

"Did my mother tell you my father came for a visit?"

"Recently?"

The surprise in her voice tells me she had no idea.

"I guess I dreamed I heard him talking to her."

"Yes," Daytime says, "that's common with an absent parent. But tell me, Elizah, why do you spend so much time at the river? That's where your mother thought you'd be."

"I like it there. Sometimes I travel around on it."

"Is that how you got to Huguenot Street tonight?"

"Yes. I took a boat."

"On a cold night like this?"

"Yup."

"May I ask why?"

"I like to be on the river. I just feel peaceful there."

"So that's what you do? You take one of the canoes down here, then you walk home?"

"Usually I come back by canoe, but this time it got too dark."

"What do you do on the river?"

"Think about stuff."

"I see," Daytime says, convinced she's found me out. "That's your place to be alone; that's very common behavior for your age group, to want to be alone like that. But tonight you're not going to be alone. Everyone should be arriving for the buffet by now."

"I know."

"I'm sure Kyle is at your house already, and also Mrs. Pensick and Mary Alice, and Brittany. Your mom said they're your two closest friends. I have to tell you again,

Elizah, not only are you doing well in Wenspaugh, but your mom is, too."

The whole time she's speaking, I'm remembering Nathaniel, how his face looked in the mirror, how huge and luminous his eyes looked, two moons inside a sky of smoke.

And how his face stayed in the mirror like a glass portrait.

✿

My mother has put ceramic turkeys all over the house; plastic cornucopias spill wax fruit. Dirk is there wearing, unbelievably, an Indian headdress. I can barely hide my laughter as he walks around the living room with feathers blooming down his back.

The house seems overheated and searingly bright, a place filled with noise and cooking smells and siren-like voices. After being on the silent river and walking through silent Huguenot Street, stepping into my mother's living room is like plummeting from the cold recesses of outer space into the middle of a Mardi Gras parade.

Dirk sees me almost immediately and walks up to me.

"There she is," Dirk says. "You gave your mother quite a scare."

"So now it's your turn to scare me with that headdress, is that it?"

My mother comes up to us. "Elizah, is this true, what

Ella says? That you were at Huguenot Street and you got there by canoe?"

I nod.

"You understand that Dirk and I are going to have to remove the canoes down by the river now. You understand that, don't you? It's just too dangerous to have you sailing off like that in this kind of weather."

"I understand," I say, thinking, what you really mean is that when Dirk helps you, it will be his first gesture of acting like a father toward me. Especially when it's announced in a public place, as if witnesses have to be summoned. Mary Alice and Brittany are standing next to Mrs. Pensick, gazing at me sympathetically.

Dirk gives me a few avuncular pats on the shoulder. This motion causes one of the brown feathers to fall from his headdress. We both watch it spin and drift onto the floor and when our eyes meet, I start laughing. He smiles.

I don't tell them how I would never consider not going to the river to meet Nathaniel, how I would never consider not going back to him.

"Elizah, I was so scared." I turn to see Kyle. He touches my elbow and through my sweater, I feel the heat of his hand spreading. It seems odd to me, now, that touch would offer heat. I'm so accustomed to Nathaniel—to the ferny coolness of his touch, to the heat that returns to my skin when his hand is pulled away.

"Sorry," I say.

"What were you just thinking about?" Kyle asks. "You

had the oddest expression in your eyes just now. I've never seen you look that way before."

"How warm your skin is, how I feel the heat. That's all."

Kyle grins. "Athletes have the best circulation. That's why my skin is so warm. It's like fire, right?"

"Right."

"Plus, I've been working out a lot more, bulking up for the season. So I'm getting even hotter now."

He leans over and I turn my head. I feel his hand still on my elbow, the outline of his ribs as he brings me toward him in an awkward hug. I stand there for a few seconds while my mother and Daytime smile approvingly. I count to five before unlatching myself from his embrace.

"I'm starved," I whisper. "Just let me get washed up and get something to eat."

"Hurry, okay?" He flashes me the victory sign, as if I'm some kind of sports goal he is about to score. I stand there for a few seconds just looking at him, standing in front of me holding two fingers in the air. Dirk walks over to him and whispers into his ear. Watching the two of them, I get the sickening sense that my mother and I are on some kind of parallel date.

I'm washing my hands in the main bathroom when Brittany stops by the open door. "So your mom was freaking before. She called my house and asked me to call Mary Alice. She had, like, this phone chain going. I think it's so cool that you went out on the river like that. I would love to do something like that, especially this time of year, but

I'm way too scared. All I would think about would be, like, drowning or freezing to death or something."

"I don't feel scared out there," I say, soaping my hands up again. "It's like I'm in another place, and it's really safe there."

"Oh God. You're like scaring me, just the way you say that. Look." She shows me how the hair on her arms is standing up. "Don't talk like that."

"But it's true. I feel like I'm going somewhere else when I'm out there."

Brittany leans a little closer to me. "Are you all right? You didn't like…smoke or drink anything on the boat, did you?"

"No. But I do feel strange whenever I'm on the water. I really do. Like I'm in a trance or something."

"I guess I know what you mean. My parents used to go out on the river and they always say it made them feel all peaceful and stuff, but I figure they say that because they were dating then, and they act all spacey about anything they did when they were dating. Imagine going out on a date on a canoe on the river. God."

"I think it might be romantic, actually." I dry my hands very slowly, one finger at a time. "It's almost hard to come back to all the stuff here after I've been there. I'd rather be there. It's, like, slower and quieter. And it's weird because when I'm here, I think about being there, but I never think about here when I'm there."

"That's weird, and I sort of don't understand what

you're saying about 'there,' 'cause the river is like three hundred yards from your house. I don't get what the difference is, but that's just me."

"It's not like that, though. It's hard to explain. It really is like when I'm on the river, I'm in a different place. Like a totally different place."

"But you don't go anywhere else, Elizah. You're just letting your mind go free, that's all. My parents always say stuff like that, so I've heard it before. It's like the river is all mystical and stuff. And it's just a river."

"Yeah. I'm not sure of anything right now. Do you ever feel that way, Brittany?"

Brittany looks at me for a long minute. "Not really. But I think I'm going back out to the party. And Kyle is probably looking for you."

Kyle. I follow Brittany, thinking how seeing Kyle gives me the same feeling as when I find an assignment sheet at the bottom of my backpack that I forgot to do: a chore that needs to be taken care of before I can go on to my actual life.

I'm standing in the kitchen eating a plate of turkey with cranberry stuffing when the psychic guy who taped the electronic voice comes over to me.

"Elizah," he says. "We've never been formally introduced. I'm Edward Bannley, and I was on the ghost walk."

"Yes, I remember you. How could I not? You thought you heard my name on that recording."

"I wanted to let you know that I've listened to that

innumerable times, and I'm quite sure there is a voice saying the name 'Elizah.' But of course I cannot say with any certainty that it's you the voice is calling. Elizah was a common name in Wenspaugh for a very long time. More common than it is now." He takes a long sip of his coffee. "But I would love to run some experiments on you."

"Experiments? On me?"

"Perhaps that's a bad word for it. You're aware that within the psychic community, there's a very widespread and accepted belief that adolescents are magnets for psychic activity. As your body changes, all that energy attracts energy."

"And that's what spirits are, right?"

"Yes, they're energy. So I've been curious: have you felt the presence of anything or anyone else since you've moved to Wenspaugh?"

"Not really." The expression in his eyes is so eager that I almost wish I had seen something I could report to him. "Sorry. Once I saw a man with long, sort of wild hair in the graveyard, but he was just walking around the cemetery after hours. Nothing else." As I say this, I realize that the man I saw that day looked exactly like the man waiting on the knoll in Nathaniel's village. In fact, the more I think about it, the more I'm certain that the man is connected to Nathaniel. But why would he walk all the way down here and wait in a graveyard?

"What?" the psychic asks. "Are you remembering something?"

"No, I was thinking about someone else. A boy, actually."

"Oh," he says, disappointment evident in his eyes. "Do me a favor, then. If you decide that I could conduct just a few simple experiments, or if you do see or experience anything unusual, objects moving, unexplained noises, take this." He hands me his card. It reads: *Edward Bannley, Gatekeeper of the Bridge*, with his phone number and email address.

"What bridge do you keep?"

Edward Bannley looks at me curiously. "I thought you would understand that," he says. "Since you live here and seem so receptive to ... well, my ideas."

"I'm sorry, I don't know what that means."

"A lot of us, you know, people like you and me and a few others here, your mother for one, believe that the dead are here, with us, as if it's just a bridge they're crossing. What I find intriguing about this idea is that some think that we, the living, seem like ghosts in their world. And with my interest, and little bit of knowledge, I like to think of myself as a kind of gatekeeper."

"Oh. I get it."

"Do you think you might be interested in the experiments?"

"I'm not sure," I say, but I know I would never be able to sit in his office and let him hook me up to wires and electrodes. "What are they like?"

"Mostly they measure the energy levels surrounding

your body. The more energy you have, the more likely you are to be … you know, visited in some way."

"Okay. Well, thanks."

"You'll remember to contact me, won't you? I have the most distinct sense that you're a clairvoyant of some sort, a person who's connected to the unseen or the unspoken. And right now, at your age, you would be at the height of your powers."

"Of my powers?" I smile. "I'll let you know if anything sort of shows up."

Connected to the unseen and the unspoken. This phrase stays in my mind as I think of my father's late-night visit, and how I can't speak of either him or Nathaniel. Of course the psychic senses that I'm connected to the unseen and the unspoken—two people in my life have to be kept secret.

Kyle comes over and gives the mild Edward Bannley a proprietary stare. Mr. Bannley excuses himself almost immediately.

"What do you think would happen, I mean really, if that guy ever came upon a real ghost?" I ask Kyle.

"A real ghost. Elizah, think about those two words together. You can't be serious." Kyle puts his arm around me in a stiff motion that reminds me of an arm frozen into position during a game of freeze tag. For a few seconds I stand next to him, stranded with a plate of cold Thanksgiving food.

"Let me get rid of this plate," I whisper.

"Elizah, you're always running off. I think it's time we had a talk." Kyle says this in a rehearsed way, his words sounding as stiff as his arm posture looks.

"Isn't that the girl's line?"

"Come right back, Elizah," he says, his voice weirdly strident.

"Yes sir," I say. "I think we better talk too. I'll ask my mother if we can go outside for a few minutes." I say this because I'm hoping Nathaniel might be somewhere by the river and I can escape Kyle.

Kyle and I walk down to the edge of the river. The night is cold and the wind smells of pine.

"Elizah, I'm just not getting any response from you," Kyle says, pulling me toward him. The roughness of his touch surprises me. I push back, but he holds me there, my arms pinned to my sides, his arms locked behind my back.

"C'mon, Kyle. I can't breathe like this."

"Relax, Elizah. I just want to make sure you don't slip away from me again. I want to make sure you're really listening to me this time. Elizah."

"What?"

"I'm going to keep you here like this until you listen to me."

"Let go of me."

He tightens his grip. Panic rises in my ribs; I close my eyes and listen to the river, trying to calm down.

"No, I'm not letting go of you. You have to listen to me. I've never felt this way about a girl before, and ... "

"You mean you could always control girls before, and I'm more difficult."

"I really like you, and when I talk to you, I feel like you're a million miles away. But not this time, Elizah. This time…"

His mouth covers mine and he thrusts his tongue in. Initially, I'm too stunned to protest, and with my limbs bound by his embrace, I withstand the jabs of his tongue, the weight of his body as he presses into mine. But I cannot breathe. I look into the sky, at the sharp points of stars, at the bright moon jewelling the darkness, and I remember Nathaniel's eyes inside the mirror, the way they looked, twin moons, their brightness inside haze. Closing my eyes and keeping the image of his face in my mind, I gather all my strength into my arms. Once I feel a slight yield in Kyle's embrace, I push back with all my might. The force of my push surprises me.

It works. I'm free of him. I taste blood in my mouth from where I bit my tongue while pushing him away. The might of the push caused me to stumble backwards and land in a tangle of brambles. When I stand up, I don't see Kyle at first.

"Kyle?"

No answer.

I run from tree to tree to see if he has plans to ambush me. While running toward a large maple, I trip over him.

He is on the ground, his left temple glistening. When I lean over, I see blood on his head, causing his temple to gleam in the cold light.

I run to get help, but before I do, I turn and quickly scan where we were standing. What I don't want to say is that I did not feel entirely alone when I pushed him from me; it was as if I had help.

ॐ

After they take Kyle to the emergency room, I explain what happened to my mother. We're drinking herbal tea and have blankets wrapped around our legs. We used to do this in Queensport whenever it snowed. Only then it didn't feel tedious.

"So Kyle didn't fall? There was no slipping on the ice?"

"No."

She looks into her tea cup, then looks away. "Did I tell you that your father wants us to hide him here?"

"Is that all you're going to say?"

"Elizah, I have no idea what is going on with you. You injure your boyfriend when he tries to kiss you a little passionately, he ends up getting stitches and checked for a concussion, and this is not information I can exactly share with anyone. So what do you suggest I do?"

"I don't know. Maybe think how I might be feeling right now. Sort of upset and worried about what will happen the next time I see him in school. Maybe ask me how creeped out I am."

"So why did you lead him on?"

I put my tea on the table between us. "You know, I have always hated herbal tea. Always. I only drank it because when I did, you would talk to me. And I didn't lead him on. I talked to him, for God's sake. I never once acted like I liked him."

"You went out with him."

"To one basketball game. I go out of my way to avoid him at school, and he acts like he owns me. Even if I did lead him on, Mom, he can't shove his way onto anyone like that. He got what he deserved."

"Maybe. I take it you two are on the outs?"

"God. Mom."

"This will put a tremendous strain on my relationship with his aunt." My mother looks out the window. "Look at that, Elizah. It's starting to snow again."

"It is."

We watch the snow for a few minutes. "So, Mom, what would you say if I told you that when I pushed him off me, I felt as if I had help?"

"Define 'help.'"

"I don't know. Kind of like an invisible force?"

"Well, I would say it was adrenaline. It's not exactly likely that the dead would rise and come to your aid for a puppy love squabble. And you didn't answer me about your father."

"Maybe that's because it's sort of your problem, Mom."

ကာ

That night, I take the bone out and put it on the windowsill. I fall asleep watching its silhouette as the snow falls.

When I wake, I decide to tell Nathaniel I found it in the graveyard. It's the first thought I have as I open my eyes.

Then I hear my father's voice in the kitchen. Quickly, I put the bone back inside its box and slide it into my nightstand.

☙❧

"I made breakfast," my mother says casually. "It's a really nice apple cobbler with vanilla yogurt."

My father hugs me hello.

"So when did you slither in, Dad?"

"Late last night." He laughs. "Nice way to put it, but I guess I deserve a little ribbing."

A little ribbing.

"So," my dad continues, the minute I sit down, "Mom tells me some boy got a little fresh with you."

I sigh.

"I think you did the right thing," he says.

"Because you would know what that is."

"Elizah!" my mother says loudly. "Go to your room this instant!"

"To my room? Mom, you've never acted this way before. Stop pretending we're normal."

"It's all right," Dad says. "She's got a point. And that's a decent segue for what I'm about to say, anyway. Elizah. I've decided to go back to Queensport and figure it all out. The whole thing. Tomorrow, I'm calling my lawyer."

I nod slowly, thinking how much I want to believe him, yet I don't. "How are you going to pay for it all?"

"Slowly," he says. "Probably for the rest of my life. It's not like I'm going to plead innocent or anything."

My mother beams at him.

"We'll talk about it more when we get back from visiting Elizah's boyfriend in the hospital."

"He's not my boyfriend," I say quickly. "Stop saying that, please. Mom, really!"

My mother winks at my father.

I turn from my parents and look out at the bluish snow. Only in my life would a mother be proud of a father for going to jail. It sort of goes along with the idea of going to the hospital to visit someone whose injury you meant to cause, and then have your parents call him your boyfriend.

I don't think things can get odder until I'm buttoning my coat and see Dirk's car drive up to the house. My mother is behind me, taking out her keys, and the minute she sees him, she leans over me and whispers, "Distract your father until I can get rid of Dirk." Then she rushes past me, nearly knocking me into the umbrella stand.

ॐ

"I can't imagine why Dirk came here," she says as we drive toward the hospital. "I had no idea he was going to show up. What would happen if Dad saw him?"

"Uh, let's see, he would know you were, like, cheating on him?"

"Cheating on him? How can you say that? We're just friendly is all. Dirk and I are only friends."

"So how does it feel when everyone else assumes someone is your boyfriend? Pretty shitty, doesn't it?"

My mother stares at the road as she drives. "Look, Elizah, I'm sorry if I haven't been very... perceptive with you or attentive lately. It's just that I've had a lot on my mind. I never meant to push you toward Kyle. And if you don't want to see him anymore, you should break up with him."

"Oh. Okay. As long as you say it's okay, Mom."

My mother smiles. "Stop, Elizah. I didn't mean it like that."

"So what are you going to do with Dirk? If Dad is going to be in jail for so long... "

"I don't know. Don't ask me now. The holidays are coming soon and the Board of Trustees at the graveyard just asked me to do a cataloging of the caskets for a booklet they're publishing on the town's history. I wasn't ready for one more minute of work, with the days I'm spending on the maintenance of the records, and—"

"A cataloging?"

"Apparently there are styles of caskets that were popular, the children's caskets, different designs, locks and hinges and all that stuff. Did you know they used to have little devices put into the caskets in case you were buried alive? If you woke up buried, you could pull this little lever and a flag would rise to alert someone that you weren't dead."

"Nice. Did they ever have a false alarm? Like a chipmunk chewed on the cord or something and the flag rose?"

"I'm not sure. But anyway, I was hoping you could help me with that a little."

"I will. Categorizing caskets is one of the ways Brittany and Mary Alice spend quality time with their moms, too."

We're still both laughing as we walk into the hospital.

When we get to Kyle's room, Daytime is there along with Kyle's parents, who look and act exactly like game-show contestants.

"Hel-loh!" his mom says, greeting us at the door. "Elizah! We've heard so much about you!" She hugs me and I realize the hug-trap is genetic in this family. For a few seconds I'm breathing only her perfume and all the oxygen disappears.

"Hey hey," his dad says, pumping my hand as if it is an oil rig. "Hey, little lady."

"Nice to meet you," I murmur.

I'm wondering if Kyle has a sister he never told me about. I thought we were both only children, but there is a girl at his bedside with thin, brownish hair.

"Kyle, how are you?" I ask.

The girl turns. It's Sidra, smiling at me with a sinister look. She makes sure the four adults are all out of earshot before she says, "This is all your fault. I should have known as much."

Kyle puts his hand on hers. "Stop, Sidra. She didn't

mean for it to happen. Elizah would never hurt me." Kyle looks up at me. "At least not physically."

"I didn't know you two knew each other," I say.

"Well, Elizah, you learn something new every day," Sidra whispers. "But apparently you hadn't told Kyle anything about your dad. Now why is that, Elizah?"

"Because I knew you would, Sidra. That's your job, isn't it? You're sort of like my publicist. Only you don't even realize how much attention and sympathy you've won for me. So thanks for that, Sidra."

Kyle smiles at me and I walk closer to his bed. "Listen, Kyle, I didn't mean for this to happen. I hope you know that."

He pats my hand. "It's not that bad. The only bad part is it's basketball season, but they said I would only miss a couple of games. They don't think it's a concussion, just a bump. Once I get the stitches out, I can go back."

"Good, that's good."

"And hey, Elizah, I didn't know all that stuff about your dad. Sorry."

"That's fine." I gesture toward Sidra. "She can fill you in on the whole thing. She's read up on it and knows everything."

Sidra narrows her eyes and, for a moment, she so closely resembles a snake that I'm waiting for her to hiss.

"That's not a good look for you, Sidra," I say. "Small eyes don't look so great when you make them into slits. They sort of disappear and it makes everyone wonder how you can see through an opening that small. It almost seems scientifically impossible, as if you're modeling the amazing capacity of the human body or something."

"Shut up," she says loudly.

A nurse comes in and asks Sidra and me to stand behind a curtain while she examines Kyle.

Sidra looks directly at me. "You know, freak, he doesn't like you. No one in our school really does. Not one person."

"Coming from you, Sidra, that has, like, so much meaning. And I think I was at the same party you went to. So much for your hypothesis."

"No, you're wrong." Sidra smiles, her lips over her teeth. "People talk to you just to see how weird you are. After you left that party in the middle of the night, Taylor said talking to you was like opening something that had gone bad in the fridge, just to see how bad the stink would be or how weird the mold might look. Like an exactly-how-creepy-can-this-girl-get kind of thing, and that's all. No one actually wants to be around you. We're just sort of forced to be around you because you came here."

"I don't think Kyle feels that way."

The adults come over before she can answer and launch into talk of pizza and soda. Half an hour later, I'm sitting with Kyle's parents, Daytime, my mother, and Sidra at a pizzeria, waiting for lunch. I completely avoid Sidra's glances. It seems she's been dropping by Kyle's house, and is also the step-daughter of Kyle's basketball coach. Sleet taps the windows while we wait for the pizza, and all I can wonder is if the river will freeze soon. If the river freezes, I won't be able to see Nathaniel.

The conversation drifts past me in the same way clouds drift past me; I know words are going by, but I connect with nothing that is being said. We finally stand, and I cannot name a single subject that was discussed at the table.

It takes Mom nearly an hour to navigate the icy roads home. The house is dark and cold inside; I know immediately that it's empty and that my father is gone.

"I never believed him," my mother says quietly. "I thought he seemed undecided last night. I guess I just wanted to believe him. He told us that to trick us."

I put the living room light on. Mom goes into her bedroom and comes out quickly, her face pale.

"I probably shouldn't tell you this, Elizah, but your father took the money I'd been saving to get you some Christmas presents. All of it. He left this note. Look. Only four words." She holds the paper out to me.

"I don't want to see it."

My mother shakes her head back and forth and reads it anyway. "It only says, 'Sorry, will replace soon.' The goddamned coward didn't even sign it."

"It's okay, Mom. We'll just have a quiet Christmas."

My mother is crying. She spends the rest of the day in bed, her door shut, the lights off.

Ice ferns the windows, and I watch it form as I lie across my bed. I hear my mother getting out of bed, banging the bed frame into the wall as she moves around. She's in the room next to me, but I can't go to her any more than I can go to my father or to Nathaniel, the people I think about the most.

I close my eyes and try to picture my father looking for a room in some invisible place where he won't be recognized. I see him looking around furtively before the image disappears from my mind.

When I think of him now, I think of the blank space inside me when I'm alone, of the way my aloneness sometimes feels like I'm standing inside a canyon and there is just wind echoing around me. I want to be angry at him like my mother is, to cry or bang beds into walls. But nothing happens when I think of my father: it's as if he's someone who was always meant to leave.

I put the bone on one end of my bed and spend the rest of the day drawing it from different angles again. I think about nothing else but the rise and slope of the bone as I put its dimensions down on paper. When I'm done, I put it on the windowsill and watch it until I fall asleep.

∾

At school on Monday, Brittany and Mary Alice rush over to me before homeroom.

"We heard that you guys were making out down by the river and got really wild ... "

"No," I say. "That's not what happened."

"And," Brittany says, nearly gasping with laughter,

"here you are, this quiet girl all the time. Like, no one had any idea you could be like that."

"Like what?"

Mary Alice rolls her eyes. "Sneaking off like that in the middle of your mom's party to make out with Kyle. Or should we say, *really* make out. He ends up in the hospital! Unbelievable!"

"No, he just slipped," I say, but no one hears me over the laughter. "He'll be back in school tomorrow anyway. They're just making sure … "

But they're not listening. I watch them laugh so hard that the hoods of their mouths are visible, their eyes crease with laughter, and they hear nothing of what I'm saying.

I think how when I met Nathaniel, one of the first things he said to me was I had to learn to listen. Last night, I listened for hours. I listened to the low moan of the river that meant ice was forming on its surface. No canoe can navigate a river clotted with ice.

And I have no idea when I'm going to see him again.

"Don't look so upset," Brittany says, putting her arm around me. "These things have a way of working out."

"Yes," I murmur. "I suppose they do."

{OƆ}

Daytime calls me down to her office at an unscheduled time. She is all serious and direct as I take my seat across from her.

"Elizah, there are two reasons I wanted to see you

today. The first has to do with Kyle, and the second has to do with your parents."

As she says this, I think how little of my life I can tell the truth about. I cannot speak of Nathaniel, or of his village; I cannot tell people about my father, or that he came and took our Christmas; I cannot say that I meant to hurt Kyle, or that I don't want to be associated with him.

"Kyle has told me that you have mixed feelings about him."

"I…"

Daytime holds her hand up. "That's fine. It's completely normal to feel conflicted about your first love."

Immediately, I think of Nathaniel. "No, with a first love, it's just that the feelings are overwhelming, is all. They're so powerful that…"

"Why, Elizah, what a lovely way to put it. I'll have to tell Kyle you said that."

"I didn't mean it about Kyle really…"

"Don't apologize or be embarrassed. We've all experienced our first love." She shuffles some papers on her desk. "But I do think it's a little unfair for your counselor to be so connected to your boyfriend." She winks.

"No, you don't understand…"

Holding her hand up, she shakes her head back and forth. "I don't need to understand any more. I think things between you and Kyle should be kept confidential. I'm probably not going to be seeing you after Christmas anyway, and since I'm Kyle's aunt, it would be best if we just let that matter live itself out in a natural manner. Unless, of course, there are major problems that you need to discuss. That would be a different story."

"So don't mention Kyle anymore in here?"

"For now."

"Okay. So what's the second thing, about my parents?"

"Your mom. I wanted to ask how you might feel if she worked here as a substitute teacher."

"Dear God."

"I'm sorry you feel that way. She's being interviewed right this minute." Daytime bites her lower lip. "She called me last night and told me that the salary the town is paying her is pretty low, and she has a sudden need to supplement your income. It won't be so bad, will it?"

I think of my mother standing in the kitchen in the baggy pants she bought at the secondhand clothing shop, in the pilled sweater with her hair uncombed, springy gray strands sprouting wildly from her scalp. Then I imagine her in front of my social studies class, standing by the globe, trying to quiet the kids down.

"I don't think she can handle being a substitute here."

"Why not?" Daytime leans forward, this artificial, tell-me-anything expression on her face.

"Forget it," I say. The bell is ringing for a fire alarm, and what I don't tell Daytime is how stupid the questions she asks are. It's not as if anything I say can stop the course of my mother's actions.

season of snow

The following Monday, snow falls for three hours straight. They cancel school for the next day, and my mother decides to bake.

"You want to help?" She stands in the kitchen, looking at me hopefully.

"I think I want to do my homework. Then I can have tomorrow free."

"You want me to save some of the baking for tomorrow, then?"

"All right. Okay if I go for a walk?"

My mother glances out the window. "Just be careful. I wouldn't want you to fall on any of the headstones and split your head open; it's icy out there."

The afternoon is cold; I step outside and am instantly aware of tiny veins constricting inside my nose. The snow has stopped, and now the sky is pinkish with bands of yellow. I walk to the river and look out at the jagged islands of ice.

"So much has happened."

I don't know whether I have spoken or someone else has.

"Elizah."

I turn. Nathaniel is behind me. We embrace for a few minutes before speaking. I feel the coolness of his skin as he puts his hands beneath my chin.

"Nathaniel, I didn't know if I would see you again or

not." I'm still leaning into him, smelling the earthy pine scent of his clothing as I speak.

"What made you think anything was finished? There are so many things that never finish."

"I don't know. I guess the snow, the weather. I wouldn't be able to get down the river in the canoe, so I just thought I wouldn't see you."

"We don't have to go anywhere. I like it here, as well."

"Nathaniel, after I last saw you, after we went to your house, did you come up here anytime? Did you come to the cemetery when I was with Kyle?"

"I'm always here." He grins. "I thought you knew that."

"C'mon, be serious. I mean here in the graveyard when I was with Kyle. Were you here at all?"

"Yes."

"Why didn't I see you?"

Nathaniel shrugs. "Will you bring what you found, next time?" He pulls me closer to him.

"What?"

"You told me you found things here, around here in the graveyard."

I put my hand to his chest to feel his heartbeat. I cannot tell if it's the pulse in my hand or the thrum of his heart I'm feeling. "Did I say I would bring it? I don't remember saying that. I think you're making assumptions about me." I lean back slightly while still inside his arms.

"Yes, I am making some assumptions. It's as if I heard you wanting to show me something the other night, or maybe what I heard wasn't spoken."

I smile up at him. "Right. I actually was thinking of showing you something I found around here, but I never told you. Maybe we're telepathically connected."

But I know I've never mentioned the bone to Nathaniel; I have never spoken of having found it.

"Yes, I think that must be it. I think we are connected in ways neither one of us understands. That is true."

For a few seconds, we stand listening to the river, to the low shrill of wind. "So if we're telepathically connected, what do you think it was that I found? Or have?"

Nathaniel takes my hand and I follow slightly behind him as we walk over to the boulder I was sitting behind the day I found the bone. Somehow I know he's going to walk there. "Elizah, didn't you find something here? A while back now?"

"Yes. I did find something here. Not long after we moved to Wenspaugh, I found something here. But how do you know that?"

"Because I know someone who wants it." Nathaniel is still standing there when I notice that no condensation escapes his mouth into the cold air.

"Nathaniel, are you breathing?"

He laughs. "What kind of question is that?"

"There's no smoke around your nose or your mouth. Look." I exhale a cloud of breath; it lingers in the air. "You're standing there like a tree."

"It must be the way the light is hitting my breath." He squeezes my hand slightly. "So, you will bring the bone next time, Elizah?"

A chill runs through me, a chill that has nothing to do with the temperature. "I never told you anything about a bone. Never."

"Elizah, we are running out of time. Please." He goes behind a tree, and I wait for a few minutes before going toward him.

"Nathaniel, sometimes I get the idea that I'm making you up. Or something. Why are you so strange all the time? This sounds crazy, really crazy…"

"Go ahead." It seems like he's speaking into my ear. "There's nothing you can't tell me. Nothing."

"Nathaniel, sometimes I sort of wonder if you're really here or not. I don't know. It's sort of like I've connected with someone who isn't there. Like right now. I know how this sounds, but…"

He comes out from behind the tree and looks toward where I'm standing. For a second his face, shadowed by branches, has an eerie, skinless look, as though he is only bone and hair.

"Nathaniel, don't stand there! You look awful. Come back over here."

He darts behind the tree and I wait for a few seconds, but he does not appear.

When I look at the path he walked to the tree, his footsteps have been buried. Snow shudders down the pine branches, and I wonder if that's how his footprints got covered up so quickly.

"Nathaniel?"

No answer. I should not have asked him anything; I've scared him away.

I wait until my fingers and toes grow so numb that I cannot feel them. By the time I walk back to the house, it's dark out. Only a thread of moon has risen in the snow-swollen sky, and its light turns the snow on the headstones the palest blue. I'm standing on a pathway near my house when I hear the crunching of snow. I turn, but no one is there.

Yet I know someone is watching me walk home.

"Goodbye, Nathaniel," I call.

When I go inside, Dirk and my mother are sitting close together on the couch.

"Hey."

"Elizah!" Dirk calls in a hearty voice. "Out walking with the spirits in the snow?"

"Maybe."

"Your mom has made some great stuff over there. Go ahead and help yourself, right in the kitchen."

"Thanks."

Mom comes over to me, as if I've forgotten where we keep our plates and cups.

"Why the face, Elizah?"

"Maybe it bugs me when a stranger welcomes me into my own home and offers me food from my own kitchen, that's all. You think he'll let me use the bathroom next?"

My mother does a rapid, twitchy dance with her closed lips but says nothing. "I would like it if you could show some respect, if you don't mind. Do you think you could do this one thing, Elizah? Do you think you could? After all, Dirk is going to help us create a holiday party." She hands me a plate of meatballs and homemade Italian bread.

"What's the deal with all these parties you're having?"

"Well, Elizah, maybe I'm making up for all the time I had to sit in the house with your father because he didn't want to have people over."

"I thought you liked us being by ourselves."

Mom sighs. "Elizah, as much as I once loved your father, you'll find that more often than not, marriages are business deals."

"Huh. I didn't think first ones were." I take the plate and a cup of hot chocolate into my room without turning around to see my mother's expression.

ω

That night, snow slides off the roof, whiting out each window for a few seconds. I'm sitting in my room and take the bone out and look at it. I'm certain I never mentioned it to Nathaniel, but I'm also certain that I connected the bone with him, with his presence, which I sometimes feel when he is not physically in the room with me. At first I thought it was only because I'd found the bone in the graveyard and I'd met Nathaniel not far from the same spot. But there was more to it than that.

He must have seen me that day, back when I first came across the bone. He'd been watching me from somewhere in the cemetery. There was no other way to explain it. The idea of him watching me from behind one of the cemetery trees or stone vaults did not scare me; I kind of liked the idea that he might have seen me before I saw him. I would have to ask him the next time I saw him.

I put the bone on the windowsill and looked out over the stillness of the graveyard. Maybe Nathaniel had climbed up to my window and seen the bone resting there in the moonlight. He could have done that. If he'd come and seen it there, and looked in and seen me, I would feel better about asking him more about his life. He still hadn't told me if his family, if that whole strangely silent village of his was part of the colonial simulations, or a religious group of some kind that did not keep pace with the modern world.

If Nathaniel had been watching me, either in the graveyard or in my sleep, I had the right to ask him more about his life. And I would bring the bone the next time I saw him. Then he would have to tell me.

∽✾∾

"Elizah, since you have today off from school, I'd like you to help me with the casket catalog." My mother comes into my room without knocking just as I slip the bone from the windowsill and back into its box. I pretend I'm looking out the window.

"Fine."

"Most of the roads are closed at this point, so Dirk is going to shovel out a path."

"You let him … stay over? Eww."

"On the couch. Don't go telling your friends any stories about us. I let him stay on the sofa so he didn't have to drive home."

"What if Dad comes for one of his moonlight visits? Slinks in though the night again?"

"And eventually finds Dirk here?" My mother shrugs. "It's not like he's coming back. At least not anytime soon." She reaches into her pocket. "Speaking of your father, I found these in a box in the kitchen."

She hands me three brooches my father and I made from the bird bones we used to hunt. I take them and place them on my bureau.

"So," Mom says, "there's breakfast on the island. I'm going to put a fire on, and then we can get started on organizing the drawings."

"They drew the caskets?"

"I think they were from advertisements. And yes, the cemetery keeps records of everything. Really, of everything, even the costs of the funeral, the casket, the burial, all of it. Death has always been a business, really."

"Like some marriages."

My mother walks over and picks up each one of the three bone brooches separately, places them exactly as she found them, then walks out without saying a word.

After I put the bone safely in my nightstand and get

dressed, I walk into the kitchen where Dirk is making fresh coffee.

"Morning, sunshine. I like your hair today."

"I haven't combed it yet."

"Still, it looks good. Very full."

"It's called bedhead."

"Well then, Elizah, I like your bedhead."

"Huh. Where did Mom go?"

Mom comes in carrying a laundry basket filled with papers. "It's kind of a lot," she says apologetically. "The Board wants all these papers organized chronologically. Most of it is paperwork from the casket purchases, bills and burial lot descriptions, but they're from all different churches in town so there isn't any one place where you can find the dates. We have to look at each paper. I thought we could begin by making piles for each decade, like the 1820s, the 1830s, then get more specific as we go along. Make sense?"

I take another bite of oatmeal and nod. She forgot to tell me that Dirk was going to help us today. I'm completely trapped today with her and Mount Rushmore.

And I don't believe for one minute that he slept on the couch.

"So then," Mom says, "after we do this for a few hours, maybe we could talk about which friends Elizah would like to invite to our holiday party. As kind of a reward." She and Dirk smile at me as if I like parties.

I look down at the first paper. It's a handwritten, three-dollar invoice for a burial blessing and prayer; attached to it are three yellowed sketches of coffins. One of the coffins has a latch that looks familiar to me. I haven't seen a single coffin since we've moved here; Mom's job is to take care of the house and the grounds, and all the burials go through an office in town that dispatches the gravediggers.

"Where have I seen this before?" I ask Mom.

"That latch? Look." She pulls two papers from a small pile. "That was really popular around the 1850s, right up to the 1870s. See these?" She points to several drawings of caskets. "Almost all the caskets used that type of latch. It's called a scroll latch, and it was made by one of the locksmiths in Wenspaugh. For about twenty or thirty years, people requested these latches."

"So I've probably seen it on houses around here or something?"

My mother looks at me. "No, I don't think so. They were specifically for caskets. Elizah, don't get upset, but occasionally the river rose and the caskets got caught in the flood and floated around the town a bit. This latch guaranteed the families that any ... you know, remains or what have you, would stay put. So no, I doubt people put this latch anywhere in their homes since it was pretty much known what they were for. Who would want to be reminded of casket latches while eating dinner or spending time with their family?"

"I've seen it before, is all. And caskets don't upset me, remember? I just know I've seen it before, and I've seen it pretty recently."

"Maybe in my office. While genealogists were there or something."

"No, I've seen it in real life. Somewhere. It just looks really familiar."

"I can't imagine where, Elizah. Anyway, do you mind doing this stack?" Mom hands me a six-pound pile of paper.

"What if I say I do mind?"

Mom gives me a silent glance and takes her basket over to the sofa.

For the rest of the morning and into the afternoon, my mother, Mount Rushmore, and I order the records of the long-dead into categories.

When we're done, we put up Christmas decorations until nightfall. All I'm thinking is that tomorrow I will see Nathaniel. And I will find out more about him right after giving him the bone.

ॐ

School begins late the next morning, and the snow seems to muffle even the classrooms, the voices, the colors. I get through the day as if I'm sleeping, murmuring concern over the bandage on Kyle's forehead and smiling at the glowering Sidra.

Mom is off to the Board of Trustees when I get home, so I immediately go down to the river. I carry the bone under my jacket and walk along the path near the shore. Every time snow falls from one of the pine boughs, I turn to see if Nathaniel is there, if he is following me or near me. I try to walk to his village, but nothing looks familiar. I'm not sure which direction to follow, how far I should go into the woods or where I should turn.

I walk back to the cemetery and wait. I was certain I would see Nathaniel today, yet when the sun begins to set on the river, I know he will not come. Still, that night I place the bone on the windowsill as if, in some strange and silent way, I am luring him to me.

ॐ

My mother begins substituting twice a week, as Daytime had warned. I hear her voice as I walk down the hall, the substitute-teacher voice filled with pleading followed by the louder voices of kids who will never listen. I walk quickly past her classroom, embarrassed by her presence.

Of course, this behavior prompts a visit to Daytime. When the pass to the counseling office comes during math, Sidra leans over and in a stage whisper says, "Well, look at that. Elizah Rayne is going to a Gamblers Anonymous meeting instead of algebra." This causes the class to burst into laughter and I feel my face burning as I walk down to Daytime's office.

This time I'm going to say anything to get rid of her and these sessions.

Daytime closes the door quickly behind me and gets right to the point. "Elizah, your mother says you will not say hello to her in the hallways."

"I don't go into her classroom, is all. I don't want to disrupt what she's doing. And I have a question."

"You know you can ask me anything, Elizah. You've always known that."

"Right. If you didn't, like, know my mom so well, if I was just like an anonymous kid here, would you have called me down here? It's just that I feel sort of uncomfortable, now that I know people and all, coming to a counselor's office. It was different when I first got here, but now I'd just rather sort of come on the sneak. Or maybe we could just talk when you come over to Mom's house."

"You know, Elizah, I'm impressed, very impressed by your maturity."

I knew she would be. I wait to hear the rest. Daytime taps her pencil eraser on the desk blotter.

"And yes, I see what you're saying. You get decent grades and you don't have any behavioral issues, so maybe it's a bit strange that you're coming here. I can release you from the counseling sessions, but you have to promise one thing."

Anything, I think. "Sure. What is it?"

"You have to promise that you will definitely come to me if you have any difficulties. Is that a deal? Even if it's something to do with Kyle, you have to come to me, all right?"

"And no more being called down here?"

"Not unless it's a real emergency."

We shake hands solemnly and I leave, triumphant that I

will never again have to sit in her office and pretend I'm normal so she thinks she can help me with normal problems.

ಬಂ

That afternoon, my mother and Dirk leave a note in the kitchen that they have gone out Christmas shopping. I decide to try and walk to Nathaniel's village, even though he said that wasn't possible. I certainly can't seem to get there by boat. It would have to be pretty much a straight walk, and it would have to follow the river's path.

I walk quickly in the early dusk, trying to locate the village by looking through the pine trees toward the river. We had gone straight down the river and docked the boat to the left.

It had been dark the one time I'd walked back through the trees and onto the road, so I'm having trouble remembering. I try looking into the sky to see if there is any smoke rising from chimneys; I listen for voices or noise of some kind, but the air stretches as blue and empty as outer space.

A group of older people touring the colonial houses pauses to look at me as if I'm part of the tour. I smile and pretend I'm intent on looking at a hedge of berries growing near the road. As soon as they pass, I dash into the woods and run straight toward the river. I should be able to find the village from there.

But there is nothing. I see the back of the Dutch church, a few gardens from the restored homes, and some rocks. I thought I'd chosen the right area of the woods, but now the sky is growing dark and the woods are filling with web-colored shadows.

"Nathaniel," I say into the silence. I listen, but there is not even an echo.

Then I see a figure up on the knoll and I run toward it, my heart pounding. The person turns and I see it's one of the older people on the colonial-house tour. He comes toward me holding a branch.

"Were you looking for some holly?"

"Holly?" I scan the buildings quickly to see if Nathaniel is anywhere. "No, why?"

"I saw you examining the berry bushes when we first got here and I thought you might be looking for some holly to make a wreath. That's how they decorated these houses for the holidays, and I found this branch just lying there on the ground. It's yours if you like. It's got a lot of berries on it."

I walk over to him and take the branch. "Thanks. This will look nice in a vase."

"It would." The old man looks at me strangely. "But why would you come down here for holly? It grows all over these woods."

"I just thought about the holly afterwards. I was actually going to visit someone in the village."

The old man pulls his hat down over his ears as the wind starts. "The village is the other way."

"No, I mean the village that's in these woods here." I

gesture toward the river. "Somewhere around here, there's a village where my friend lives. I just can't find it."

"There's no village here, honey, except for Huguenot Street. There's just the restored houses, a small pine forest, and the river. The only other village is about half a mile up the road, and you can't miss that one, with the streetlights and stores and all."

"Oh," I say, turning toward the road. "I guess I'm mistaken."

"I think so. I've lived in Wenspaugh all my life, and there hasn't been a village by that river in over one hundred years or more." He laughs. "You must be new here."

"Yes. Well, thanks for the holly." I walk quickly toward the road, away from the senile old man.

∞

Three days pass. The snow turns dirty. In school, I have to be asked questions two and three times before I can answer. I feel foggy, distant from everyone around me. Dirk has not left the house since we catalogued the old burial records and caskets; around him, my mother speaks in a bright voice that breaks frequently. I try not listening to her, complaining I have too much homework, but I dash off most of my homework on the bus. It keeps Beth Mooney from speaking to me.

"You're so quiet," Beth says that morning. It's a cold Friday, the last day of school before Christmas break. Mom and Mount Rushmore are hosting their holiday party tonight, and I'm yoked to them like a boat to an anchor. There is no chance that I can see Nathaniel. And he's the only thing I can think about. I have not seen him since that afternoon by the river.

"I have a lot of work to do."

"I can't do work on the bus," Beth says. "I'm too distracted by all the noise. You have great focus to be able to concentrate. Not me. A bird chirps and I forget everything I am reading and totally lose focus."

"Interesting."

Beth waits a few minutes, which is unusual for her. "So what's going on with you and Kyle?"

"I just say hi to him when I see him and kind of ignore him now."

"Oh. Because I saw him with Sidra at the video place in town. And she said, 'Be sure and say hi to Elizah,' and I thought you should know that."

"Okay." I close my science book. "Sidra just doesn't get what bothers me yet. She's doing me a favor by keeping Kyle occupied."

"The thing is"—Beth spins the end of her hair nervously—"that Kyle called me over to the table and asked me to find out what's wrong. He meant, like, with you, why you're so quiet and sort of far away in school now. You should have seen how mad that got Sidra. Her face was blazing red."

"That's the thing, Beth. I just want to be alone now. Nothing against Kyle."

"Just so you know, everyone thinks not going out with him is crazy. He's, like, amazing. I'm just saying."

"Don't they already think I'm crazy?"

"Not anymore," Beth says. "Only when you first got here. Now everyone knows you're just like the rest of us. Just a little more quiet 'cause of what happened with your dad and all."

"Right."

The bus stops. Beth vanishes into the line of loud, talking kids. I slip into the group, then quietly run to the side of the building where I can cross over into the woods. No one calls my name, but my heart is pounding as I walk. I'm moving so quickly that my backpack bumps painfully into my ribs. My mother and Dirk are out shopping until at least noon, and the school doesn't call to report absences until after one o'clock. Maybe I'll see Nathaniel if I can get to the river clearing this morning. I don't know why I think he'll be there, and the whole thing seems crazy, but everything in me is telling me to go there—to the spot not far from where I found the bone—and meet him.

Everything.

I stop at the house to get the bone, still nestled inside its box. When I get to the large rock at the river's edge, I'm panting. My lungs ache and my thighs are thrumming with the strain. I duck down behind the rock and sit on my backpack just in case Dirk is taking Mom for a quick drive around the cemetery before they leave for their shopping. Two birds land in opposite pine trees and their weight causes snow to skitter into my hair.

I'm brushing it out with my gloved hands when hands close over mine. I shut my eyes.

"I knew you would be here."

Nathaniel laughs. "Good. I was trying to send you mind messages. You got them."

"I don't know. I'm skipping school. When my mom finds out, I'm dead." I stand and turn to face him. "I'm hoping I can erase the message before she hears it."

"But you were listening," he says. "That's how you heard me. I knew you would learn how to listen. You always could."

"I guess. I'm not sure I always could." Nathaniel moves closer to me. The mingled scents of pine and earth rise from his jacket, and I lean into his body and put my hands on his shoulders, feeling the solid width of them.

"Elizah, I was never supposed to have feelings for you here, not during this time."

"Because your parents only want you to be with people from their cult or their village? Is that what you mean?"

Nathaniel leans down, pressing his lips to my cheek. The familiar coolness spreads across my skin. "I have to hurry," he whispers. "I am almost out of time. Did you bring it?"

"You mean the bone?" I pull back slightly from him, bringing my hands to his ribs.

"I do. It's for someone who has to ... continue on. And you have it."

"I'm feeling really confused right now."

"This will all make sense to you one day."

"God. If I give the bone to you, will you tell me how you found out I had it? And why I couldn't find your village?"

"I will answer you as best I can."

"As best as you can. I guess that's better than nothing." I slip away from him and get the bone, still in its box. Before turning to give it to him, I take one last look.

"Here. It's inside this box."

Nathaniel embraces me. "You have no idea how much this means to me, to us all. No idea."

"Uh, right on that account. I don't. So how did you know I had it in the first place?"

Nathaniel puts the box in his coat pocket. "Because I felt it when you found it. We all did. All of us from our village did. And about the people I'm with—"

"So it is a cult of some kind? You don't believe in electricity or phones or things like that?"

"We are a specialized group of people, yes. We can only be seen when we choose to be seen. Do you understand that? Please say you do; I have only a few more minutes."

"You can't explain anything more to me?"

"Not details, but things you would understand. Elizah—what would you do for your father?"

"For my father?" I smile. "I'm not too sure, since he doesn't really ask much of me. He's not around."

"But if he did ask something of you, something that seemed impossible, would you try to do it for him?"

"My father." The air is cold, stinging my nose as I breathe. I think of my father, of the way he looked standing there in the darkness, like a person haunted. And I feel no anger or sorrow, just a familiar pang.

"You would, wouldn't you?"

Nathaniel is looking down at me. His eyelashes graze the top of his brow bone.

"I'm not sure. But there are other people I'd do impossible things for." I meet Nathaniel's gaze, wondering if he knows I mean him. "There are people I would do the impossible for, yes. I'm just not sure my father is one of them."

"But you understand, then."

"Yes."

"I'm so sorry, Elizah. There are things I want you to know...there are things I will tell you that I cannot tell you now. All I can say is that you and I were meant to meet, and you already know more than you realize. You just have to listen. Then you can remember the rest."

"Those aren't really answers, Nathaniel." He opens his arms wider and I press myself into him. "And what do you mean, I will remember the rest?"

Instead of answering, he kisses my cheek again.

"Nathaniel, are you coming back?"

"Here? Yes. I will come back, but not with words. I will be silent. I came here to help my father. I think you understand that, somehow. Now my father has words. Because you have given them back to him."

"You will not come with words." I repeat this and close my eyes so he doesn't see how I'm beginning to cry.

When I open my eyes, he's on his way to the river. I walk quickly after him to the knoll. The wild-haired man is waiting inside the strangely shaped boat we used last time we went down the river. I watch Nathaniel hand the man the box with the bone inside. It's the last thing I see before Nathaniel turns to me and waves goodbye.

I hold my hand up as they navigate through a fragile lace of ice coating the river. As they push around the bend, the sun kindles the red stain in the boat's wood, and I see the latch.

Nathaniel spins around and looks directly at me, just at the moment I realize what I'm looking at. That latch is the one that was specifically used on caskets.

I put my hand to my mouth as Nathaniel turns away.

He and the man are drifting down the river in a boat made from a casket. I traveled with Nathaniel in that same boat the last time we went to his village. We'd floated down the river inside a casket.

I stand in the cold air listening to the silence ringing around me, too stunned to move.

∽∾

At home, I wait for the school to call, and right after they leave the automated message about my absence, I erase it. I'm looking through the papers we organized that day, with the burial records and the caskets, since I'm certain that boat was made from a casket. The mahogany wood, the brass designs, that latch...that latch only used for coffins.

Why on earth would Nathaniel do such a thing?

I hear Dirk and my mother drive up. I quickly take my coat and backpack and go into my room, where I will spend the next two and a half hours in my closet so they don't find me. Out of habit, I go to my nightstand to take the bone out, forgetting that I've already given it to Nathaniel.

For almost three hours I sit in darkness, thinking about the coffin-boat, imagining what Daytime would say if I told her I loved a boy who did such things.

If he even was a boy.

ဢ

After I hear the bus drive up, I have to put on my coat and backpack and sneak out the back door, to pretend I've been at school all day.

Dirk greets me at the front door. He has reindeer antlers on, with tinkling bells at the ends.

"Getting an early start," he says, by way of explanation.

"Right. You look like you're wearing a giant branch on your head."

My mother walks in holding a tray filled with glasses and holiday plates. "I've had these since forever but I never used them with Michael. Your father was such a loner." She winks at me. "Wasn't he, Elizah?"

"He probably still is, unless he's dead."

"All right, that's enough, young lady." My mother begins putting the glasses in order on a table decorated with sprigs of holly. "Maybe you could help me a little over here?"

I'm relieved that the usual "how was school?" and "did you see Daytime today?" questions are not asked.

"So Mom, do coffins float?"

"Dear God. Elizah, can't you please ask me normal..."

"I'm serious. Like, could a boat be made out of a coffin?"

Mom is placing a ceramic Santa in the middle of the table. "You ask such cheerful questions, kiddo. I don't know. I guess they could float. They float down in New Orleans after the hurricanes and floods all the time, and I know they floated around here when the river crested, because it's in the cemetery history. The gravediggers used to put stones and heavy objects on the lids just in case. But I've never heard or even imagined making a boat out of one. This sure qualifies as one of your odder moments."

"So it's possible?"

"I guess. But the better question is, why anyone would want to do that when a log would make a perfectly good boat? Now stop, Elizah. We're going to be celebrating the Christmas season in about an hour and a half and you're definitely giving me the creeps."

I look at my mom, fretting over arranging a vase of silk poinsettias, and I want to say, imagine how I feel, having ridden down the river in a casket to a village no one can find.

But instead, I go and change into a red sweater and jeans, acting as if this party is the main thing on my mind.

∞

Mom is standing in the kitchen, organizing shrimp into a circle. "I hope you don't mind that Kyle showed up."

I shrug. "Like I can do anything about it."

Kyle is busy talking to Daytime at the dining room table when I go back out, and Daytime waves me over. She is holding a package that I'm hoping is not from Kyle.

"You weren't in school today," she says, and I look around furtively to make sure Mom isn't within earshot. "And Sarah Poulle gave me this to give to you. She said you'd been wonderful about helping her in the science room."

I take the wrapper off: it's a book about Wenspaugh legends.

Daytime reads the title. "She said there was one in particular you would like, something about spirits returning, and that you would know what she meant."

"Yes. I remember talking to her about that. Thanks for bringing it."

"You still are into that stuff?" Kyle asks.

Daytime scoots away from the table to talk to Dirk. I look at Kyle.

"Yeah. I like that stuff. Legends, ghosts, all that. I think there may be something to it."

"I thought you were, like, into science and not nonsense." He says this in a sneering way.

"Science is considered nonsense before they can prove it." I spear a shrimp off one of the trays my mother has left on the table. "Think of all the beheadings and imprisonments there were when people came up with theories that went against popular belief. And Kyle," I say, backing past him, "you would be the type who would send Galileo to the towers, behead Newton, and fling Madame Curie into a convent. Exactly the type."

Kyle opens and closes his mouth, then says nothing. I walk away from him and sit on the sofa next to Mr. Bannley, the ghost-walking guy who had the gaussmeter and wanted to do psychic experiments on me. Brittany and Mary Alice group around Kyle and give me curious glances.

"How are you?" Mr. Bannley asks.

"I've been better."

"Sorry to hear that," he says. "Anything I can do to help?"

I look at Mr. Bannley, at his wild shrub of hair and his grateful expression that someone has landed next to him at the party, and I shake my head.

"You have a book?"

"Yes, from Ms. Poulle at school. It's on local legends and some of the town history."

"Ah. Wenspaugh has always had so many legends."

I'm wondering how long I'll have to sit next to him when he holds up a small booklet. "This is quite fascinating."

I see that it's the catalog the town has printed from

the records my mother, Dirk, and I organized. It's a thin magazine that I can't imagine anyone being interested in reading. Ever.

"Why do some people think death records and casket styles are fascinating?"

Mr. Bannley laughs. "I guess they tell their own stories."

Kyle orbits me twice, but I pretend not to notice.

"The joke about this little booklet is, 'the facts that we dug up.'" He grins. "If you can live with that pun."

"Oh. Right. But I think they got all the facts just from old papers."

"I know, but did you know they used to put the days on the graves? Say someone died at age forty-six. They put forty-six years, three weeks, and four days. Isn't that something? Time was measured differently then."

"Huh." I lean back into the sofa, wanting the party to be over. Mr. Bannley thumbs through the booklet. "Myself, I listen to the legends, but I put my money on finding energy fields."

"I like the legends more than the records."

Mr. Bannley nods. "But records are stories, too. Here, see this one here? This grave, there's a drawing of it. Ah! Got it!"

I know that as soon as he's done speaking, I have to find a way to escape.

"The Mathias graves, here. They lived in this house once, did you know that?"

"I didn't."

"Your house has been here, in some form or another, for over a hundred and fifty years. It's been added onto a few times, but the foundation, the basis, has been here almost since the beginning of the graveyard. Some of the Loomis clan lived here as well, many decades ago. I'm not sure which ones, but it would probably be on a census."

"Wait. The Loomis family?"

"The Loomises married into the Mathias family, but when they left Wenspaugh, we lost their trail. I think they scattered."

"I know a Nathaniel Loomis in the village."

"Well, they left town over a hundred years ago, so I don't think he'd be related."

"But he's named Nathaniel Loomis. I know him. His parents are, like, part of the colonial simulations, or they're in some kind of cult. They live about a mile downriver."

Mr. Bannley shakes his head. "I'm sorry, Elizah. I do the records for the town historical society. There hasn't been any village down there for a century. There are some ruins, and the restored houses up higher on the embankment near the bridge, but there are no houses there. You must be thinking of somewhere else."

"No, I was there. In Nathaniel's house."

"Impossible," he says matter-of-factly. "If you like, I can take you right now to the Loomis graves, to the family plot."

"Now? It's pitch black out."

Mr. Bannley laughs. "Elizah, I'm a ghost hunter. Do

you think I'm afraid of the dark? Get some flashlights and we'll take a walk."

My mother protests at first, and Kyle reaches for his jacket, but I smile and nod, assuring everyone that we will be back in plenty of time for the cake and desserts and that we are fine by ourselves.

The night air is frigid; wind blows from the river and stinging bits of ice are mixed into the wind. Mr. Bannley and I walk to the river's edge with our flashlights. He stops not far from where I used to meet Nathaniel, down a few yards from where I found the bone.

"Here. The whole family is here. They were Dutch, and the great grandfather was some kind of preacher, out to convert the Lenape Indians for a time. But then almost the whole village was wiped out, the original one that was built closer to the town, and the great grandfather got medicine from one of the Lenape sachems. That story is in the town records."

"So he's buried here?"

"No, he's buried back where the first village was. But his son is here, daughters, nieces, cousins; there were a lot of them. There were four Loomis brothers originally in the town, and who knows how many sisters. Here's a Loomis: Obediah Loomis, infant, 1868, four weeks, three days. His sister must have died with him." He shines the light on a tiny concrete plaque: "Mathilda Loomis, 1884, aged two years, six months, eleven days. Sad, you know?"

"Yeah. But the boy I know is much older than they are."

"Nathaniel? Is that his name?"

"Yes."

"Here you go. Nathaniel Loomis, son of Jacob, 1887, aged seventeen years, three months, and one week. That's the only Nathaniel Loomis who ever lived in this town."

"No." I shake my head. "They just don't know about him because he's not registered for school or anything like that."

"I'm sorry, Elizah, but there are no remaining members of the Loomis family in this town. There was a terrible accident, where a Loomis father died while out hunting. Awful. Something went wrong with the gun. After that, the family moved lock, stock, and barrel from this town and never looked back. But they were here for hundreds of years, and that's why they figure so prominently in Wenspaugh history."

Mr. Bannley turns his flashlight off the Loomis headstone. "You can read the burial archives and see the death records right in your mother's office. It's all there, if you look in the 1880s or thereabouts. I don't remember the exact date, but that's about when the last of the Loomis people were here. So your friend may be a visitor from somewhere other than here."

"But what if he just borrowed that name from the headstone? He could have lied about his name, couldn't he? Especially if he was sneaking away from his parents, if they didn't want him like hanging around anyone not in their cult. He wouldn't want me trying to find him, or telling people I'd had contact with him. So he told me the wrong name."

"He could have, this boy. But if what you're telling me is true, that you know his name, that you went to this village...maybe you weren't dealing with a human at all." Mr. Bannley clasps his hands together. "Elizah, what if you had contact with a ghost? It's possible, you know. Very possible."

I sigh. "No. He wasn't a ghost. He was a regular boy who lied to me and didn't even tell me his right name. That's all. The whole thing was based on a big lie. Although I did feel...sometimes...that he wasn't really there. And I felt so odd when I was with him, like I was dreaming or floating." I shake my head. "But that was probably just me; it probably had nothing to do with him at all."

Mr. Bannley smiles. "Maybe. But the village—you saw that?"

"I did."

"Then you'll show me where it is?"

"I can't. I'm not able to find it. I've tried, but I can't remember where it is. And he wasn't a ghost, even though that would explain a lot. I touched him, and he had a human body, shoulders, arms, everything. And he spoke."

"Did anyone else ever see him?"

"Yes. At his village they saw him. There was a man, and a child. People were in the houses around us, so yes." I start walking back to the house. Mr. Bannley follows. "You probably think I'm crazy right now, Mr. Bannley, but

I did not imagine this boy or the village. I saw him more than once. In fact, I saw him earlier today."

"When is the next time you'll see him?" he asks.

"Never. I know I'll never see him again. I can feel it. Besides, he told me that if I ever told anyone about him or his village, he would vanish. But it doesn't matter now. He's already gone. When he left with... that must have been his dad that he left with. I'm guessing it was his dad."

"It's possible that I may have a crude photograph of that family in the archives. No promises. But if you were to see a picture of him, even a grainy one, would you be able to recognize him?"

I nod. I don't want to argue that Nathaniel was not a ghost. And I don't want to speak anymore, because I don't want Mr. Bannley to know that I'm crying.

The next morning, my mother and Dirk bring me breakfast in bed.

"You weren't feeling well last night," Dirk says, "so we thought we'd pamper you today."

"I'm okay." I sit up, hugging a pillow to my chest.

My mother stands at the foot of my bed, frowning. "So is that why you didn't go to school yesterday? What were you doing? Hiding until three fifteen, then pretending you were getting off the bus?"

I nod. Daytime must have mentioned it. Or Kyle,

Brittany, or Mary Alice. The problem with being around people is all the talking they do.

"Elizah, what you did yesterday was a form of lying. There's something going on with you that we need to talk about. I've spoken to Ella and she agreed to keep you for some additional counseling sessions after school starts again in January."

"God. Mom. Can you please stop? Daytime doesn't do any good because I lie to her. And I always will. I grew up lying. I do it really well now. God forbid if I told her the truth about Dad or anything like that."

"Ella knows about your father."

"Not all of it. Not the visits. Not the Christmas money robbery."

Mom bites her lip, and I am immediately sorry for saying this, since I can tell by Dirk's expression that he had no idea my father has been here or that he'd stolen money from us.

I look out the window. Cold mist curls over the tomb-stones, and for a few seconds I think I see a shape inside the mist. It could be either my father or Nathaniel. I keep watching, waiting for a person, a form, to emerge. But none does.

I turn back to Dirk and my mother. Dirk wears an entirely neutral expression. He doesn't know how secrets shape my life: secrets, and ghosts, and silent forces that live inside shadow.

I can't tell him, or anyone, about my father. And I

can't tell anyone about the only boy I ever liked. Not one person. Two people who have mattered to me run through my life now like an unseen yet forceful electrical current.

Dirk sits on my bed. I find this gesture amazingly forward and pull my legs up, away from him.

"Elizah, you know I'm a guidance counselor."

"Yeah. So?"

"Elizah! Be polite!"

"Why? I don't owe him anything. You do."

My mother leaves the room, slamming the door behind her.

"Maybe I can help a bit here," Dirk suggests. He's still sitting on my bed even after I have pulled my legs up so violently. "You know, I really do understand what you're going through."

"Doubt that. For one thing, you're a guy."

"It's not easy for your mom. You know that, Elizah."

"But for me, it's what? Just terrific, right? Dad's behavior forces us to leave like gypsies in the night, then I get stuck up here where it snows forever and all we do is sit in the house and have parties with the rest of the Wenspaugh misfits. And whatever happens, I'm just supposed to accept it and be all cheerful about it. And when I'm not cheerful, I'm supposed to be feeling sorry for how bad my mom has it. That's the deal, right? Oh, and attend counseling sessions where I have to hide half my life, so they do no good, then I have to go back to class and make up the work I missed and be all fine with that. It's all forced on me."

"And then there's me." Dirk says this quietly.

"Yup." We lock eyes for a minute. "Then there's you."

"Elizah, you'll find that I'm not such a bad deal."

"I think I'm the one who's supposed to figure that out."

He taps me on the knee before leaving, and after he's gone, I slide the deadbolt across the door.

At least Dirk knows he's a deal and not a choice. Two days ago, I saw him writing the check to pay Mom's Visa bill.

The snow begins a few minutes later. It snows all day and into the evening, and I lie in bed, not asleep and not awake, until my mother calls me for dinner.

That night, I decide to go through the burial records after my mother and Dirk go to sleep. I want to read them for myself. I sit though a long dinner of Swedish meatballs with some kind of minty sauce that results in the meatballs having a strangely incongruous flavor, like garlic mingled with ice cream. I'm polite and interested in Dirk's shockingly dull story about his Grandmother Swenson's recipe and how when she got dementia, she almost served mothballs. I laugh at the appropriate places and I see my mother look at Dirk gratefully, as if the stiff little conversation between Dirk and I this morning has transformed me.

I just want to get the evening over with so I can read the archives in her office. When they finally begin nodding over their books while we're sitting in the living room, I'm overjoyed.

"Elizah," Dirk says, "it's getting late."

"But it's Christmas break," I say, airily. "And I want to stay up and read some more."

Mom kisses me, and Dirk pats me on the back as if I've just scored a touchdown. I wait until their light goes out before entering the office.

It's cold in the office, which is only a glassed-in porch with some furniture and a tiny space heater that my mother turns off at night. My fingers begin going numb as I search through the papers. She's in the process of transferring the records to the computer, so the piles are fairly organized. It only takes me a few minutes to find a folder marked 1866–1886. I carry the folder back into the light and warmth of the living room.

Mr. Bannley was right; there are over one hundred Loomis names in the folder. Some of their birthdates go back to the 1830s. The same names keep appearing: Mathilda, Matthew, Obediah, Jacob, Jane, Sawyer, Hannah, John, Josiah, Ezekiel, Mary, and Elizabeth. The causes of death are usually listed: fever, accident, childbirth. I sift though about thirty papers before I come across Nathaniel's name. It matches the tombstone. The paper reads: *Nathaniel Loomis, aged seventeen years, three months, and one week. Died of the prevailing fever, January 30, 1887, son of Jacob Samuel and Margaret Rose Deyo Loomis.*

There is no other Nathaniel listed in the records. Maybe, I think, the records are incomplete. There could be graves that were unmarked, other relatives of this large family named Loomis.

Wind blows and loosens slabs of snow from the roof. I listen to them fall. His footprints. The coolness of his skin. The boat fashioned from a coffin. His strange way of speaking. The image that stayed in the mirror after he turned away. The way the light sometimes left his eyes, his skin. How there was no cloud from his breath in the cold weather. But all of that could be explained; tricks of light, the way he was standing, my own strange languor when I was with him.

I open the records again and search his family. His father is there: *Jacob Samuel Joseph Loomis, died 44 years, two weeks, and four days of gunshot wound.* Gunshot wound. But his mother, Margaret Rose, is not there. She must have moved away when the Loomis family moved on, moved away from Wenspaugh. She was not buried with her husband and children. Their bodies were left in Wenspaugh.

I close my eyes. I want to dream of him, but instead I dream that I'm lost inside a blizzard and cannot find a way out. The more I walk, the deeper into the dangerous pine forest I go. When I look up, the sky is growing darker.

Never once does my sleeping mind form Nathaniel's face.

He haunts me only when I'm awake.

∽∾∽

I wake before my mother and Dirk, the death records spilling all around me. I'm just putting the last ones in place when I hear Dirk fumbling in the kitchen, making coffee.

"You're up early," he says.

Mr. Obvious notices something.

"Yes." Quickly, I escape to my room.

An entire day with snow, my mother, and Dirk. Nothing to do but listen to them scurry about the house making sounds like rats trapped inside a wall.

I start leafing through the book that Ms. Poulle gave me, about the legends of the Shawangunk Mountains. There are a lot of legends about names, about how your corn and apple crops can be bewitched, and a lot of herbal remedies with weird names like wormwood, skullcap, mad weed, or bridewort, that can be made or eaten to ward off crop failure, backache, or irritability. I'm about to put the book back on the shelf when I see the legend Ms. Poulle had spoken of that day in the lab. It's called "Reclamation." According to the legend, reclamation was a common occurrence in Wenspaugh.

The belief was that after the body died, the spirit rose up and if anything was missing from the body, such as an arm bone or a leg bone, the spirit got trapped in mists over the Shawangunk Mountains and would not be able to walk or carry things in the afterlife. It was a hybrid legend, a mingling of the Lenape idea that after death the spirit went on a journey, and the Christian belief in ascension after death. The author went on to say that the spirit had to return in human form to retrieve what he or she needed to complete the journey. And the only way a living person ever knew there had been contact with the dead was through a small gift that would be left behind.

It matched the story Ms. Poulle's grandmother had told her. I like the idea of ghosts walking among us, dead among the living, looking for what they needed to go on.

I think of my father tapping on my window, of the way he came to us like a spirit. But my father was alive, and he didn't leave us a gift: he took a gift for himself. Yet somehow we were all connected in this, in a journey where we touched each other, even briefly, then went on.

I'm not sure our journeys ever end. The legend seemed to mirror this conviction.

I look at the book again. The next passage is about the living person meeting with a Council of the Dead. I've just started reading it when Mr. Bannley comes to our door. Mom acts surprised that he wants to see me.

"Elizah, I found the picture in the town records. Of Nathaniel Loomis. It's not terribly clear, but I thought you might want to see it."

Mom looks over. "Who is Nathaniel Loomis?"

"It's like ... just something I'm interested in. It's sort of ... like history."

"Wenspaugh history," Mr. Bannley adds.

Mom nods, then goes into her room to wrap presents. My hands are shaking when Mr. Bannley hands me the fragile paper. The corners of the photograph are webbed with lines and the scent of dust and disuse rises from the page, but I see Nathaniel right away.

It's unmistakable. His eyes, his hair, his mouth.

"There must be some kind of mistake," I whisper.

"This is Nathaniel, but he wasn't light or energy or a spirit of any kind. He was real."

"I went there," Mr. Bannley says. "To the village you went to, the one along the river. You said it was about a mile downriver, and when I matched that up to this family's address, I found exactly the site you were talking about. There are only ruins of homes there, Elizah. Some bricks from foundations, the remains of an old well, but no houses. Nothing."

"I was *in* Nathaniel's house." I'm still holding the picture. "There were beds and cups, dishes on a hutch. I saw the house; I sat at his family's table." I don't tell him I tried on his mother's necklace, or that we watched ourselves inside a mirror. "The house had all the things a family would need."

"I think I know what's going on here, but I never thought I'd see it. And if I did, I never thought it would happen here in Wenspaugh. Elizah, would you mind if I wrote a paper about this?"

"I don't care." I hand the picture back to him. "Maybe I can read your paper and then I can understand what happened. Because right now, I feel tricked."

"You're friendly with Sarah Poulle, aren't you? Your science teacher?" Mr. Bannley puts Nathaniel's picture back and shuffles papers around inside his folder.

"Not friendly, really. I mean, I like her and I help her out at school and stuff, but it's not like I ever see her here like Mrs. Daytner."

"I used to teach science at your school, and I called her last night. I hope you don't mind. She told me you had shown her sketches of a bone, of a human jaw bone, but she didn't seem to think you actually had that bone in your possession." He looks up, his eyes brightly hopeful. "Do you have that bone?"

"I had a bone, yes, and it was a jaw bone. But I don't have it now. I gave it to him. Or to whoever that boy was. I really don't know what's going on now. Not at all. "

"Elizah, would you be willing to go with me, back to the village? Just for a short time. I'm curious to see if I could pick any activity up with one of my instruments."

"Fine," I say, and slump down on the couch.

"You know Elizah, none of this seems to scare you. Not a bit. That's unusual. Do you think it's a little frightening that you might have had contact with a spirit?"

I shake my head. "That stuff never scared me, spirits and bones and all that. I'm way more scared of the living."

"Very nice," Mr. Bannley says. "Very nice. This will work out perfectly. I'll ask your mother if we can take a little drive."

Of course, Mom lets me go with Mr. Bannley. He explains there might be psychic activity of some kind and she thinks we're researching the Loomis family. Ever since Dirk came to live with us, Mom only half listens to anything anyone says.

We're standing in the exact spot where Nathaniel's house was, and it's true—there's nothing there. A few pine trees, bricks, a scatter of stones. Mr. Bannley runs his gaussmeter over the area, stopping to jot notes down. I watch him for a few minutes, then walk closer to the river's edge.

"What about his father, Nathaniel's father? Did he die here, in the hunting accident?"

"Jacob. No, it was up behind the house you live in now. He was trying to get some deer down by the river. They say he died while cleaning his gun. I remember that one." Mr. Bannley shakes his head. "Jacob Loomis got half his face blown off in the explosion. I think that was the main reason they left the area after that. Margaret lost three of her children, then that accident, losing her husband like that. I believe she had two other children, young ones, so she went back to her family a little west of here."

"Half his face blown off? How do they know that?"

"Records. They buried him with a closed casket. There was no way the undertaker could fix that man with the bottom half of his face missing."

"So he was buried … incomplete?"

"You bet he was. Poor man."

"So he had no … jaw?"

"Oh, this sounds like one of those legends." Mr. Bannley smiles. "Sarah Poulle always knew the legends. I don't put too much faith in them, Elizah." He taps the gaussmeter. "This here tells me all I need to know."

Vultures circle the mountain; the old farm is shuttered by snow, and the air rings silent. I'm sure Nathaniel's house was in this spot; I remember looking out the window at the farm. Then I remember … I didn't see the farm when I was inside Nathaniel's house. The river was there, the mountains, but when I looked north, through the window, there had been no farm.

"Mr. Bannley, when did that farm get built? Like what year?"

"Oh, you mean the Gustafsons'?" He looks across the river to the snowed-in farm. "That's been here since about 1910 or so. Long time now."

"Did you pick up any activity?"

"Yes, strangely enough, more than in the graveyard." He looks over at the farm again. "Why do you ask about the farm?"

"Because I just realized that when I was with him, the boy, I only saw the farm when I was heading back home. On the way here, I never saw it."

"Is it possible you never looked? Had an absentminded moment?"

"No, I like that farm. I always look. I just didn't think to look when I was with him." I sit down on a cold, flat boulder. "It was like I was in a kind of trance when I was with him. Not a trance, but like everything else fell from me, and it was just me and him."

Mr. Bannley smiles. "That sounds more human than anything else." He returns to his gauges. I listen to the wind until my feet and hands grow numb.

"I'm freezing," I say.

"All right. But I think I'd like to take one of the rocks from here, just as a kind of touchstone."

My mother invites Mr. Bannley for lunch.

"This is exciting," she says, and Dirk nods, sort of like a ventriloquist's dummy. "To think there might be some kind of activity going on just before the holidays. But Elizah, I'm surprised at you, such a rock-and-bone kind of girl who likes science."

"Lots of people who believe in the supernatural have backgrounds in science," Mr. Bannley points out.

"Do you believe in it, Elizah?" Dirk asks.

"Not sure."

"And you obviously do," Dirk says to Mr. Bannley.

Mr. Bannley takes the rock from his pocket. "Well, let's say I don't believe in the spirit world in the same way I believe that this is a sedimentary rock. But I also know that we cannot explain everything about energy. What makes certain cells come together and begin life, that spark? We don't know all there is to know about that. And what happens to our energy after we die? How does it change? No one knows. The nonbelievers don't know anything more than the believers. I'm just looking for a shred of proof."

Snow swirls outside.

"Right now," Dirk says, "I'm just looking for the snow shovel. That path is going to be covered by sundown, and it will freeze."

"I'll help you," Mom says. "We'll be back in a few minutes."

After they're gone, Mr. Bannley looks at me. "I think that boy transported his memory to you, Elizah. That's what I think."

"That explains nothing to me. That he 'transported his memory.'"

"It's a theory, sort of like being inside someone else's mind. He showed you what he remembered: his house, his village, all of it."

"How … so none of it existed, but it had a physical dimension?"

"That's right," Mr. Bannley says. "So the boy had a physical dimension, too. You were inside him, looking at things as his memory directed you."

"I was inside him?"

"Mentally," Mr. Bannley explains. "It's a phenomenon that's been documented before. It's called astral projection, astral travel. But this is a bit more than that. What happened is you went to him, you traveled to him. I'm offering that idea as a possibility to explain what may have happened. But there's so much we don't know, Elizah. So much more we don't know than we do."

⚘

That night, when the house is quiet, I open the book Ms. Poulle gave me and go back to the reclamation legend. I scan down until I come to the passage where I stopped. It says, "… *a representative of the soul, or an escort, may come back to the living if that soul is not whole, and the escort must contact the finder. The escort must bring the finder to a Council of the Dead, so that the connection between the living, the found object, and the dead can be established."*

A Council of the Dead. I look up from the sofa at the three Christmas stockings my mother and Dirk have hung over the fireplace and I remember Nathaniel's house, the fireplace that gave no warmth, the mirror that captured images. No Council of anything there, only shadow and silence.

Then I recall the circles we made around the houses, the way the people came to the windows with candles. Could that be, was that, a Council of some sort? Had those people been dead? They'd looked directly at me, at Nathaniel.

I close the book.

There are so many things about Nathaniel I cannot be sure of. I know he existed; I simply cannot explain the basis of his existence.

And he is gone in the same way my father is gone, in a strange, inexplicable absence that I understand will end one day.

I know, somehow, that I will see them both again. There's a strange comfort in the idea that my connection with both of them is not over.

I get up to close the door to the office, to stop the draft coming in. Strange, since my mother always closes the door to save on the heat bill.

I listen to the silence for a few more minutes, making sure my mother and Dirk are asleep. Then I get my coat and go into the cemetery, back toward the river where I first found the bone. I can hear the slow running of the river, the scurrying of animals beneath the low-lying ferns. I shine the flashlight on the spot where I saw the bone. The snow glows phosphorescent under its beam. I move the light in an arc, wondering if Nathaniel has left any sign behind, any message for me.

Nothing. I sit on the boulder near where I found the bone. The stone beneath me is achingly cold. I want to stay there just few minutes, remembering Nathaniel, remembering the way he looked, the coolness of his touch, then the warmth. The air smells of smoke and pine and wet soil...the scent I associate with Nathaniel.

I walk back, convinced of nothing. I do not understand what happened; I simply know I loved Nathaniel, and where he had once been is empty now. I stop at the tree where the branch had fallen across my path, last fall. I shine my flashlight on the trunk, where the *E* and *Z* were.

Quickly, I brush snow from the trunk and bits of bark shed from the tree. As the bark falls away, I see my full name there: *Elizah*. Written clearly. Beneath it, dug deeply into the tree, I see the initials *N.L.*

Nathaniel Loomis.

Did he carve my name into the tree? Or had the initials been there for decades? Were they different people?

I put my hand on his name and close my eyes. When I open them, I see a small glimmer inside the darkness, a spark of jewel dangling from a spindly branch. I reach for it and close my hand over the necklace, the gold one with the rose at the bottom, the one that was Nathaniel's mother's, that he had once given to a girl and once clasped around my neck.

"Nathaniel, did I always know you? Was I that girl?"

I wait, as if the silence will answer me.

I turn and look behind me, at the snow, at the stillness of the graveyard, at the bright orb of moon sharp in the winter sky. And I know.

He left the necklace for me so I would remember. So I would know.

He left it so I would keep listening. So I would remember to listen until I found him again.

Acknowledgments

For the creation of this book, I would like to thank Andrew Karre for both his ability to envision the unwritten and his subsequent trust in me, Brian Farrey for his perceptive reading and handling of his inheritance, Sandy Sullivan for keeping my earthbound time and space parameters intact so I could move beyond them, Marissa Pederson for her generosity in sharing her expertise, and Lisa Novak for her seamless translation of language into art.

In addition, I would also like to thank my family for listening to months of ghost tales and facts without ever once suggesting that I might need to see someone.

About the Author

Anne Spollen lives on the Jersey shore with her husband, three children, and six rescued pets. She has published extensively and her fiction and poetry have been nominated for the Pushcart Prize. Her first novel, *The Shape of Water*, was released in April 2008. She is currently at work on two other novels.

For over twenty years, she lived in New Paltz, New York, where *Light Beneath Ferns* is set. Her house was beneath the Shawangunk Mountains and across the street from a rural cemetery. She can't be sure she has never spoken to a ghost.